Iltday

by Tim Boiteau

FENRIS
™

This is a work of fiction. All characters, events, and locations portrayed within are fictitious.

ILTDAY

Published by Fenris Publishing
Flagstaff, Arizona
https://www.fenrispublishing.com

ISBN 978-1-62475-180-6
Printed in the United States, United Kingdom, or Australia
First trade paperback edition: July 2023

Cover art by Tabs Abernathy
Edited by David M. Sula

Dedicated to my grandmother and first writing teacher
Edith O'Hara (1908-2009)

Foreword

From: Dr. Carla Wen
Date: August 10, 1998
To: Dr. Alan Jefferson
Subject: Requested Document
Attachment: iltday.doc

Dear Dr. Jefferson,

Regarding our previous phone call, attached is the manuscript my patient Skeet Jeffcoat Deveaux wrote while under my care at the Midlands Memorial Hospital. My assistant transcribed it from the original, which was written in crayon and barely legible; she has attempted to preserve each and every idiosyncrasy of his writing style. I hope it proves helpful to you.

Sincerely,
Dr. Carla Wen

Chapter 1
Sunday

It took me a while before I could accurately describe the color of Sunday.

A few summers back when Gumma was still alive we all drove down to Myrtle Beach and I got the worst doggone sunburn you've ever seen. Beet red and I was howling with pain and itchy as all heck and then a few days into it my skin started bubbling up and then it peeled off and if you were very careful with it you could pull off a whole sheet. Pale and translucent. Well I kept the skin for a year or so wrapped in a couple of paper towels and when I took it out later it had grown cloudy and gray and finally I had the right word for Sunday: molted-skin gray.

Sunday is like that like it's a skin all over everything this dead gray skin. If you move too quickly it crumbles off you then grows right on back. But if you move careful-like you won't disturb it you live within the layer of Sunday and smell it too the old skin smell.

It's nice actually. It's comforting.

Well the skin I collected has long ago turned to dust because I took it out too much to touch and examine it. And what was left of it in the drawer in my room is now probably washed away in the ruin that used to be our home.

Reminds me of *The Wizard of Oz* how at the beginning everything was in black and white and then exploded into vivid color and then at the end when Dorothy returned to Kansas all the colors were drained out again. Sunday's like that. A gray beginning and a gray end.

This particular Sunday I wake up on a wet mattress at the base of a crater of ruptured wood frames and warped siding and roofing tile peeling off like fish scales. Above us is a broken sky and fast-moving clouds lingering on the tail end of Hurricane Danny. It's all gray I tell you the molted-skin gray of Sunday. Even Deidre Thomas the girl my neighbor whose hand I now hold from now until the hour of our death Amen she is all gray too except for her black hair and the black smear of blood on her face. Her eyes have gone way the heck up into their sockets so that you can't see the green anymore.

You can really look into someone's eyes when they're rolled up like that.

Don't have to look down at their sneakers the way you usually do.

I reckon we'll see the doctor today and get her taken care of and then things can go back to usual except that now we'll finally be living together.

I'll also be talking to the police I reckon.

That's okay. Talked to them before and it was all just a big misunderstanding. Hot diggity. Maybe they'll give me more Atomic Fizz Neon Lime Flavor (Fear the Fizz) and chocolate-frosted custard-filled donuts from Dunno Donuts like last time.

"Well" I say to Deidre Thomas. She's got drool coming out of her mouth as she lies next to me on the mattress. I swat the mosquitoes away from the wound on her head and the gray of Sunday crumbles apart and rains down. "I guess we best be getting up. Lots to do today."

Chapter 2
Monday

It's Monday eye-melting orange and I stop writing when the scratching in the attic starts up. A persistent sound. Hard to think straight with it scratching away like that. Hard to get my studies done. I don't work Mondays as a general rule unless chores and studying—which is what I call writing in my notebooks—are work (and Gamps says they're not) so I'm home to hear the scratching.

I go to tell Gamps about the scratching because he's the expert on things like this and he doesn't like me poking around the attic where he's got all his war memorabilia stashed away (it's a pull down and he says my fat *ss will break the wooden ladder). Don't know if I mentioned that I'm bigger than Gamps. Got about a foot on him and he says I got danged boats for shoes they're so big. I was taller than him by thirteen the lankiest danged thirteen-year-old he'd ever seen. And now I'm twenty-one and still growing.

Gamps usually complains that the pain in Stan aches worse on Mondays than on other days so I think it must be important about the scratching starting on a Monday but wouldn't you know it the pain doesn't seem to be too half bad for Gamps today. He's just sitting up in bed watching the Happy Value Shopping Network wearing his favorite t-shirt which is black with motorcycles and skulls on the front and I'm wearing my favorite t-shirt too which is

Swiss-cheese white and a kitten says "Hang In There!" on the front
which is pretty funny if you think about it 'cause it looks like the
kitten is going to fall off the shirt.

Gamps's leg is off leaning against the bed and stuck into
a sneaker. That's Stan. Titanium Stan. It has this habit of always
staying inside shoes. You ever poke your head around the house
looking for Stan you will never find him outside of a black sneaker
with velcro and scuffed all to heck.

"Gamps?" I say.

"Yeah." He doesn't look at me standing in the doorway. Sometimes Gamps can't bring himself to look at me.

"There's something scratching around the attic."

When he doesn't respond after ten seconds or so I repeat myself
a couple more times before I get something out of him.

"H*ll" he says at last. "Must be another squirrel."

"I reckon so."

Gamps keeps staring at the television—it's sixteen color inches
rolled up to the foot of the bed so you could crawl over the covers
and through the screen into the stage where a pretty lady in a red
dress her skin all aglow in the blinding orange light of the TV stu-
dio shows off her 100% real guaranteed genuine colorless diamond
ring-necklace-earring combo set.

"Guess I'll go up there and take care of it" I say.

"Like heck you will. Let Gamps handle it."

Gamps hasn't been in the attic since the... actually he's never
been in the attic on account of his metal leg which prefers solid
ground thank you very much. Gumma was the one that did all the
up and down. Back in the 80s during Hurricane Hugo—which if
you didn't know was a Category 5 hurricane and powerful enough
to uproot a mature pine tree and hurl it into our roof and shake
everything with a terrible force—I was scrunched up in the tub
with a bunch of pillows (that's what you do during hurricanes even
if you are too danged big to fit in a tub). My teeth were vibrating and
the frosted windowpanes got smashed clean out then the rain flooded down through the pull down and warped our ceiling in places.
Gumma was the one that went up after the storm and hung tarps

around the hole to divert the rain 'cause even after the hurricane there was persistent rain for a few days. Our neighbors' house at the tip of our cul-de-sac—that's a term Gamps uses but in a laughing jokey way 'cause he says it's a generous fancy-pants term to use for a dirt road—well that house was crushed completely by another pine bigger than the one that shot into our roof and the family there were crushed to death beneath the wreckage and after the rubbish was hauled away by the city no one else built on the lot. Now it's just scrub pines poking up a lot of them taller than me after all this time.

That was Hugo.

A terrible time but also wonderful because Gumma was still alive. If you stand in our front yard as I often do and stare at our house you can see that the coloring of the roof tiles is off. A patch of them fresher than the rest. It was a clean and neat shot you could say. Very little evidence of damage from the outside.

I stand there in the bedroom doorway listening and listening over the blare of the television for the sounds in the attic. Don't hear anything now. Maybe because we've been talking about it and maybe the scratching doesn't like being talked about or it likes scratching when no one's listening. Couldn't say. It could be a squirrel or maybe something to do with hurricanes a storm echo perhaps a bit of it trapped in there and stirring back up. That's where we're at right now in the attic investigation.

"What the h*ll you doing there boy?" Gamps says with that irritated tone he gets when I linger a bit too long in one place.

I'm listening I think.

"Skeet?"

"Yessir Gamps I'm listening."

"Well listen somewhere else. I'm working here."

"Yessir." I hesitate. "You gonna buy that 100% real guaranteed genuine colorless diamond ring-necklace-earring combo set?" It really glitters in that exciting Monday orange.

"I might just. Probably could appreciate."

"All right then."

I stand there listening some more and watching Gamps watch TV.

"You gonna go look for that scratching now?" I ask Gamps.

"D*mn it Skeet. Get out and shut the d*mn door. I'm not proper."

He means his leg. Whenever he says "I'm not proper" Stan's off.

Chapter 3
Tuesday

Tuesday now according to my daily calendar which offers me daily meditations a calendar I scooped up out of a trash bin. It's stained brown and has the perpetual sweet smell of the coffee that soaked through leaving the pages stiff and all stuck together. When I peel off the top sheet the daily meditation gets all torn up: "Take time today... up... off..."

I couldn't tell you what it was supposed to say but it's definitely Tuesday yes Ma'am that banana-yellow rubbery Tuesday and the scratching's at it again.

Up. Off.

Must be that meditation has something to do with the scratching up there in the attic.

I go in to see Gamps and he's watching Happy Value Shopping again and lo and behold if it isn't the same doggone 100% real guaranteed genuine colorless diamond ring-necklace-earring combo set that was on yesterday and that same model glamorous and sparkly and white-toothed presenting it though everything is tinted now in the yellow light of Tuesday. I watch from the doorway for a while before Gamps notices me and asks me what the h*ll I'm gawping at.

"It's the same 100% real guaranteed genuine colorless diamond ring-necklace-earring combo set from yesterday isn't it Gamps?"

He grunts.

"Did you buy it?"

"Did you hear me on the phone yesterday Skeet?"

I think about it a minute. Gamps didn't leave the bedroom yesterday from what I could remember. And I didn't bring him the phone either. "No I don't reckon you did."

"Then I hadn't bought it. Not yet anyhow. Still mulling over the prospect in the old noggin."

"Gamps."

"Yeah?"

"There's something in the attic. Scratching around." Sounds like a single fingernail running slowly but firmly down a piece of wood scraping and juddering a bit. Then occasionally it turns frantic and fast. Something really wants to get out or in or up or off.

Gamps grumbles. Don't know what all he's saying.

"If you want I'll head on up there and see what's what?"

"I'll handle it. Shut the danged door would you?"

"All right Gamps."

I stand there listening to Gamps through the shut door.

Wondering did I eat breakfast already or not?

I go and find on the counter a pack of Bubba Joe's (Hear That Sizzle) Ultra Thick Cut Bacon opened and airing and not too many flies and some defrosted lukewarm Waffacombs Now With Super-hex Syrup Pockets. They got the clever slogan "Waffa Matta With You?" And in the commercial there's a lady making Waffacombs for two kids and when she serves them up the kids' eyes go all wide and form into the shape of Waffacombs and the Superhex Syrup Pockets are dripping syrup all down their faces and the lady says "Waffa Matta With You?" I'm not sure how the commercial ends because I always shut my eyes when it comes on it's so danged scary but they're a tasty breakfast food that's for sure.

First I put the bacon on a plate and microwave it—soon crackling and popping and smelling delicious—then put four Waf-facombs Now With Superhex Syrup Pockets into the toaster oven. I mean the operational one. We got a few stacked up on the counter in Iltday red or chrome or milk white but either the springs aren't

working or the cords are frayed or what have you. Anyway. One of
the darned Waffacombs is all burnt up 'cause it had slipped down
onto one of those metal heating bars you're not supposed to touch.
It'd probably still taste all right with plenty of syrup and butter and
with bacon too.

All in all it's a pretty good breakfast and gives me plenty of
energy. I eat it with a cup of Willy Nilly's Brand Chocolate Milk
then stare at the empty plate for a few minutes and decide to make
another breakfast. I microwave the rest of the bacon and toast Waffacombs Now With Superhex Syrup Pockets. Also I brew Gamps
his Calders French Roast Coffee. When it's done I prepare the
coffee how Gamps likes ("Cream no sugar thank you Ma'am") and
take two plates on a tray into his room.

I stand outside his door listening. Still watching Happy Value
Shopping. Haven't heard him calling about that set but he'll get up
to it around noon I reckon.

I knock on the door.

"What the h*ll you want?" He sounds muffled through the
door.

"Gamps I got breakfast for us here."

A pause. "What you got?"

"Bubba Joe's (Hear That Sizzle Ultra) Thick Cut Bacon and
Waffacombs Now With Superhex Syrup Pockets."

"Is that it?"

"Yessir. And butter and maple syrup. And your Calders of
course."

"'Best Cup Is *Every* Cup.'"

I mouth that part silently right as Gamps says it.

"All right Skeet. Come on in then."

Gamps grunting and shifting his big belly poking through the
bottom of his t-shirt sits up so I can set down the tray for him then
I get another tray from behind his nightstand and we settle down on
the bed and eat our breakfast together.

"They still parading around that diamond set" Gamps says
nodding towards the TV.

I nod and stuff a waffle in my mouth.

"Take sensible bites Skeet. You gonna choke yourself eating like that." He looks like he's about to start yelling at me and pop me a good one so I look down at my plate and hope maybe the anger will pass. Sure enough after a moment Gamps pats my shoulder and says "It's all right Skeet. Hey there thanks for breakfast." He laughs. His beard shivers when he laughs and his belly too. There's not a sound I like better than Gamps's laughter. It's deep and rich and it just gives me this wonderful warm feeling like nothing else can.

I laugh too and some waffle falls out of my mouth and I quickly pluck it off the blankets. "Sorry Gamps."

He doesn't care. He laughs even harder. He laughs till he's breathless and then tells me real serious that he's about ready to buy that there diamond set.

"It's a good idea Gamps" I say.

"Darn right it's a good idea. A smart investment. Not too expensive either. Believe I'll get three. We can work that into our budget. Finish up and get me the phone would you?"

I'm glad he's in a good mood so I give him my last waffle and confess that I already ate my breakfast. When Gamps's in a good mood I sometimes use the word h*ll as in "Aw h*ll I already done ate anyway." I do this now and Gamps gives me a slant-eyed look and then chuckles.

"Skeet Jeffcoat Deveaux what would Gumma say hearing you talk like that? Get me the phone would you?"

"All right Gamps."

"And quit stomping around! Shake the danged house when you move!"

I grab the hall phone that's plugged into the wall the one that has an extension long enough that you could take it into any old room in the house if you had that notion. We have several hall phones but three of them aren't operational at the present moment and another four aren't plugged in at the present moment but the dark-red one is so it'll do the trick. I hand Gamps the phone.

"And get my wallet while you're up and about."

"All right Gamps." I stand in the middle of the room looking around.

"Well hop to it. It's in the bureau behind the TV."

I start searching though I'm not sure what he's talking about—

"Not the pinewood bureau nitwit. The one in the corner there." Right. The pinewood has a gun stashed in the upper cabinet a 12-gauge pump-action shotgun which I can look at but not touch unless Gamps has had over five Brewsters (Another Brewster For You Sir) at which point he may let me pump it a few times and do Arnold Schwarzenegger impressions.

I go to the other bureau which is a white one and why he didn't initially say the white bureau I could not tell you Ma'am and find his wallet up top in the drawer where we keep special papers from the Bank of Carolina which is where we go when Gamps gets his disability check or pension in the mail and I get my Movie Mayhem check. We rake it in pretty regular Gamps and I do. That's what Gamps says whenever we get our checks on the same day which happens more regular than you might think.

I bring him his wallet and with spectacles perched on his nose he goes through his cards and then clears his throat and rehearses how he'll talk to the sales people at the Happy Value Shopping Network call center who are pretty nice people all in all and always ready to help out. He uses a special voice for such occasions like someone on TV would which makes sense I suppose since he's talking to someone on TV. He picks up the headset and dials and shoos me away. Tells me to shut the door then apologizes into the phone saying that he wasn't talking to them he was talking to his grandson and is this Yolanda. "Oh hi Yolanda wonderful to hear your sweet alto again dear it's Jasper Deveaux that's right."

Gamps goes on talking but his voice grows quieter and quieter and more and more distant like I'm listening to him from deep inside some long endless tunnel and there's another voice inside here a voice much closer so close against my ear I can almost feel its tickling breath.

—*Please please*—

Then all of a sudden the sound switches back in clear as day.

Someone's calling my name. Don't know how long they've been calling me.

"Skeet!"

"Yessir Gamps?"

"You standing outside my door again?"

I look around a little bit dizzy and sure enough I'm in the hall outside Gamps's room. Well it's the hall outside my room too. And a few other rooms at that. A narrow hallway crowded with cabinets and boxes and odds and ends the wallpaper peeling where you can see it behind all our treasures.

"Yessir."

There's a pause. A few seconds pause.

"I got that set. Bought it off Happy Value Shopping. Three of them."

"All right Gamps." Which set? The the. The. Jewelry. Yes that diamond ring-earring-necklace combo set 100% guaranteed.

"Reckon I'll celebrate with some Brewsters I do believe."

"All right… 'Another Brewster For You Sir.'" I started sweating at some point. My face is soaked with it. It's streaming down my back. My eyes are burning and the color of Tuesday has grown more intense than usual everything coated with a rubbery yellowish sheen. The AC isn't working no no not at all and all the vents are blocked up by all the things crammed into this hallway this household. God there's so much of it. So much stuff. It's pressing in on us. Suffocating. It'll it'll—

"Go on out back and get me a six-pack Skeet."

I start to move feeling disoriented not sure where to go where to look what's happening where am I whose feet are these but then things seem to snap into place the objects in the hallway and me among them.

I huff it out to the backyard. The daylight is dizzyingly dazzlingly powerful and the air is thick with a clinging humidity that makes yellowish sweat stains. There's a carport back here full of all kinds of stuff. Lawn equipment and bicycles and all kinds of interesting bits and bobs. A little tricky to go crawling around 'cause things are always crashing and falling when I bump through them but in the back of all these treasures are the refrigerators. Got about one two three four aw heck we got a bunch of danged refrigerators and a couple of them working too. The smallest of them I stuff vegetable scraps and other leftovers in every now and then. It gets flies and maggots and stinks to High Heaven in the summer like now if you open it and sometimes other kinds of insects come around to investigate my project. Then there's the beer fridge which is full of Brewsters. Every shelf even the ones on the door and the drawers are filled with them too. It looks like something out of a commercial like this fridge appears out of nowhere steaming with cold and glowing blue and then a tiny butler with a frosted mustache pops out and hands you a beer and says "Another Brewster For You Sir."

Indeed steam pours out of the refrigerator when I open it though it's banana yellow today as you might expect and there's no tiny butler to hand me the Brewster. I cool off in the open door for a few seconds then I grab a six-pack and bring the beer in for Gamps.

Leave the beers on his bedside table and go to my room.

Spend some time shifting around my mattresses lining them up around the walls and piles of clothes. Then run into them and bounce off the walls for a good while. I call this Bounce House. It's a kind of game I suppose you'd call it.

Got about ten mattresses I'd say. Gamps told me once that all my mattresses stank to High Heaven and that they couldn't get any sunlight through my narrow-*ss window so I dragged them out back and hosed them down and let them set in the sunshine for a time. Few hours I'd say. Then dragged those heavy suckers back in and wouldn't you know it next thing I knew fire ants were crawling this way and that. Gamps got pretty sore with me about that not to mention the fact that he says I didn't let them dry properly. "Who the h*ll told you to hose down the Christ-forsaken mattresses in the first place?" he'd asked. Well it was Gamps who had told me they needed cleaning but I didn't want to hurt his feelings about it so I didn't say nothing and took my dressing-down like a grown adult. Afterwards there were puddles all in my room and the moisture warped the floor beneath the carpet and it was all mildewed and rank. I laugh every time I think about that.

We did get the mess cleaned up eventually. Never did quite conquer that smell though.

Yes Ma'am that's here to stay.

Soon I can't see straight and my head is spinning and I can't breathe and Gamps is pounding on the thin walls yelling "What the f*ck you doing in there you gonna bring the whole house down Christ Almighty why do you test me why do you test me with this boy take me now take me now I've had enough of it already enough enough enough!"

Once I've caught my breath I slide one of the mattresses aside. Here's my desk and all my books filled with stories each one that I wrote. I got about nine hundred million now I do reckon Skoolbrite Notebooks written with my collection of 10-Color Pens. I keep all the used pens in several boxes in my closet which is pretty full by the way. You can't walk in there but you might could climb over the clothes if you were small and I'm not. I only use up the yellow and green and sky-blue inks and purple and pink and orange and gray also. Black and midnight blue are unused and I only use red on occasion on account of Iltday being so uncommon but the other colors I use regular for their days of the week.

My notebooks are stacked up all over in what Gamps calls towers and I reckon that's not too far from the truth. He and Gumma bought me a bookshelf years ago before I started attending Pinehouse High School Class of '95 Staying Alive but I filled it up quick and then started stacking my notebooks on top of it and then beside it and then in the closet and well by now they're just about every which where. Mostly college-ruled. Gumma stopped buying me wide-ruled once the bookshelf filled up. She said she was proud of all the work I did in the notebooks. All my studying. Gumma said studying was work. Unlike Gamps. She would read them from time to time and laugh at some of the things I wrote in there or sometimes she would get in fights with Gamps over something. Gumma taught Language Arts at the Pinehouse Middle School so she knew everything there was to know about writing.

I take a peek out the window to see what's happening outside and see my neighbor the girl Deidre Thomas just now coming out back to read a book in the fresh air and wearing her black hair in pigtails like Dorothy Gale in the Merry Old Land of Oz. Maybe I haven't mentioned that Deidre Thomas is the most beautiful girl of all time and I don't care what Russell Lingdenberry says which is that she's only a 6 or maybe a 7 if he was feeling generous.

Deidre Thomas was Top Ten in our Pinehouse High School Class of '95 Staying Alive and was voted Most Talented because she played the saxophone in band and piano too judging from what I could hear next door though I have not heard music coming from her house in years. Also she won an award for a painting she did of the tobacco shed on top of a little hill in an old field behind our houses one of the best paintings I ever saw painted in the reds and blacks of Iltday. Whenever I walked down the halls of the high school I always made sure to stop and stare at that painting for as long as possible. Stare at it till things seemed to be moving inside that shed.

I was voted Best Smile and sure enough there is a picture of me with a big smile on page 133 of the yearbook smiling big enough that you can count all my teeth. In Deidre's picture she's holding a paint brush and her saxophone and smiling only a half smile. I think they told her not to smile too big or else people would wonder why I was Best Smile and not Deidre Thomas. I probably could have been Most Talented as well considering all the notebooks I've filled up but maybe you can't be two things so I'm Best Smile instead.

Anywho it's convenient she's come out to study 'cause I was going to do my studies too so I pull up a chair and take out my latest notebook and practice writing things. I have more education than most on account of the fact they kept me an extra year to work with Mrs. Kelly in All-Star Class where we learned all kinds of interesting lessons such as the importance of making eye contact and not just staring at people's shoes. Though I do prefer looking at shoes. Especially Dorothy's fancy ruby slippers though I wish they were a different color. Reckon it's because those shoes were Iltday red that the nasty old wicked witch wanted them so darn bad.

Tuesday today so I click out the yellow tip of my pen. It's more lemon than banana but it's close enough. Tuesdays are irksome because of all the yellow. You can't hardly read the stories that come on Tuesdays.

Write my name a few times. Got to really carve the paper with the pen so you can see the yellow. Dig yellow trenches out of that paper. Then move to sentences with my name in them and before you know it I get to writing a whole story about me and Deidre Thomas and Gamps living together and making Waffacombs and how I buy a brand-new Belleville sedan and drive everyone to Myrtle Beach so she can read books by the ocean and Gamps and I can sit on the sand and drink iced tea and watch Happy Value Shopping on the portable and we buy her three 100% real guaranteed genuine colorless diamond ring-necklace-earring combo sets.

In between writing when I have to think up the next thing to say I sometimes take a look up to make sure Deidre Thomas is still outside studying along with me.

She's pretty hardworking actually.

She works at my favorite restaurant called EAT which I like 'cause it's a pretty good name for a restaurant and which I like also 'cause they have bacon and pancakes which is a little different than the Waffacombs we eat at home and different than how Gumma made pancakes and also when they put the butter on your pancakes it is in a little ball and not in the shape of toast like we have at home and actually tastes better that way and looks different when it melts and leaves a dent in the middle of the pancake stack if you can wait that long which I can't hardly do unless a hand reaches out across the table nails painted the color of her Thursday pine-green eyes but if I try to look up at them they veer off to her left ear where she's got three silver earrings and a little freckle—

"Skeet? Skeet? Skeet?" It's not Tuesday anymore but long-gone sky-blue Wednesday set inside a Tuesday-yellow frame.

"Yes Ma'am?" I'd said.

"You were off staring" she'd said. "Tell me. Can you? Tell me. What you saw that night. Please tell me." Inside all this blue is a flicker of red. Days nested inside days like one of those little wooden dolls.

Then I'd looked down at the trail of melted butter in my pancakes.

The hole left behind.

The butter melted that time. That. Time. She held my hand.

End of my studies I got sweat dripping down my nose staining the paper in translucent yellow-edged blobs. My hand dragging across makes a whole mess of the writing but anyways you couldn't barely see it beforehand so I reckon it doesn't matter much.

Besides Gumma's not around to read my stories anymore.

Sunlight is. Different. It's changed the shadows slanting the wrong way.

What was I writing about anyway? I think and squint back at the jumble of letters swimming like tadpoles. Here's my name for several pages. Then the story. Right. A story. It's a pretty good one too but I didn't come up with an ending. I look out the window for my neighbor the girl Deidre Thomas. Out back it's empty and the windows of her house have the shades pulled down except one narrow one which has a crack of window uncovered but I can't see her there either.

It's okay. I can think about the ending until I do some more studies after dinner and maybe finish up the whole thing and give it to Gamps for his advice. Gamps is good at all kinds of things such as Happy Value Shopping and fixing toilets and giving me advice about my stories. He knows when a story is bullsh*t and told me that some of my stories were bullsh*t and that he couldn't read half of it anyway.

Maybe it will end up being published in the *Pinehouse Chronicle* on the front page and next to it a picture of me wearing my favorite t-shirt and standing with the mayor Mrs. Jessica Donaldson.

I sign my name at the bottom just in case someone comes along and wants to steal my story and put it in the newspaper with their picture next to it wearing their favorite t-shirt and standing with the mayor 'cause that way no one would believe they wrote it 'cause "Hey! Skeet Jeffcoat Deveaux already signed his name on it and what *gives* Mister you're not Skeet Jeffcoat Deveaux!"

I go to Gamps's room with my notebook and knock on the door but there's no response. "Gamps? Gamps? Gamps? Gamps? Gamps? Gamps? Gamps? Gamps?"

No response.

"Gamps? Gamps? I got something here for you to read."

I stand there listening for a while but sure enough he's out or asleep. Don't hear the TV either.

That's when the scratching starts again.

It's slow and dragging. Then it stops a moment and continues. Moving down the hallway from the kitchen and towards the pull down. Takes about a minute I guess before it reaches the pull down and then starts scratching quick and fast and relentless. Coming from the attic. No mistake.

—*Please please please*—

A woman's voice or maybe a child's.

"No" I say. "No."

Gamps told me not to go opening the pull down. Not to. Pull the cord. Unfold the ladder. Climb up there. Likely as not to break the ladder or burst through the ceiling. Then there'd be heck to pay yes Ma'am.

I guess sometimes a house has got noises in it. Nothing new. Last year we had a squirrel running around up there and neither of us went up to flush it out. It scurried around for several days and scratched at the pull down something incessant but by the end of the week you couldn't hear it anymore and then a smell started up worse even than my mattresses and that whole to do. Yes this was about the worst thing you could ever smell. Gamps had me walk down to the Slash Spree and buy all of the Lolly Pine air fresheners by Auto-Nu and well they only had a box of a hundred plus fifteen on the shelf and I got them all and we hung those trees all over the house about twenty per room but the fresh tree scent didn't quite cover up the squirrel smell. As we were hanging up all the trees Gamps said said said he said it was dead up there. The squirrel he meant. Couldn't find its way back outside. A real dang shame. And it's a shame we used Lolly Pine air fresheners by Auto-Nu on account of whenever I smell that particular tree scent I get all queasy and once even threw up but that's better than being a squirrel trapped up there in the dark suffocating heat and not able to find a way out.

This doesn't sound like the squirrel though. I don't reckon.

This sounds bigger.

Like a. Like a. Like a. I don't know what.

I run over to the den all the TV sets shaking on their stands and peer outside into the carport. Well Gamps's gone and took the Hamtramck pickup out for a spin. It's a 1979 in forest green with a V6 engine. Did I mention that already? That's what Gamps always says anyway. Not pine green but. Close. He let me drive it down to the end of the street once and I knocked Ms. Elsworth's mailbox sideways and after that Gamps didn't let me drive anymore and we hightailed it out of there back down the road and parked the truck and pretended we hadn't been driving and then a few days later when I told Ms. Elsworth when I saw her in the yard when I was out walking down to the Country Store for an Atomic Fizz Neon Lime Flavor (Fear the Fizz) and a two-foot Jacked-Up Jerky and pack of Hog Wild Crispy Cracklins BBQ Flavor I told her how sorry we were about her mailbox and she was terribly confused at first and then piping mad and said she'd have a word with Gamps and that "You did the right thing Skeet Jeffcoat bless your heart young man." This was a couple years ago around that time that they found Ms. Elsworth's dead body after Hurricane Allison. They found her dismembered and decapitated which is a fancy way of saying that her arms and legs and head had been pulled off. And Gumma too. Gumma back then. She was.

It was a big mystery around here. All those people. Part of the mystery of it was that the police couldn't find a lot of the dismembered parts. If you can't find something you're looking for you better believe you got a mystery on your hands.

I switch on the television and click onto Jerry Springer who is talking with a skinny man in big baggy jeans who's missing one tooth and has a gold one too saying that he's a changed man Jerry and won't Doreen take him back on account of the baby and all and Doreen is a big girl with blue hair over her eyes and pierced lip and very energetic everything seems to quiver when she talks. I turn up the volume to the max level so I can't hear any more of the scratching. Then I put on the radio too and turn Rush Limbaugh up to the max level.

It's not enough not quite so I go to the kitchen and there's a Lumovox TCDX-5 Boombox in there with our tapes. I click it on and Billy Ray Cyrus winds up singing "Achy Breaky Heart" which is a pretty good song and one of my favorites but it's still not loud enough to cover up the scratching.

I rummage around and find my Azimuth W-2046 Personal Portable Recorder and Cassette Player with Built-In and External Microphone and Stereo System and play the tape in there which is a recording of me watching *The Wizard of Oz* and commenting on it with Gamps snoring in the background. I turn the volume up to max and hear my voice saying "That there's Mr. 'If I Only Had A Brain' Scarecrow and what's nice about him is that—"

Still not loud enough. Not nearly.

I return to the den and sit down and think.

I could do it. Open the pull down and climb up there. Up. Off. Or I'd just open it and let the squirrel or whatever it is scurry out. I don't want another squirrel dead up there. God the smell. It's powerful. It'll take over everything. It will get inside you and won't ever leave. You smell it everywhere even where it couldn't possibly be. I still smell it I think. Sometimes. It hangs off me like an extra dead arm you can't touch or see but can smell the rot of.

Just then I decide I'll go ahead and just crack it open a bit and I go and stand under it and look up at it. The paint's peeling and bubbled on account of the accursed humidity. Our whole ceiling's that way with popcorn always falling on me and Gamps and I don't mean the edible kind.

I reach up and get the knob of the dangly cord in my hands.

"Skeet Jeffcoat Deveaux what you doing boy?!"

Gamps is in the hall hobbling towards me with his cane and red in the face. "What's all this d*mn racket? You were going up there after what I told you? Well talk boy or are you dumb as well as a d*mned moron?"

"Nosir."

He pops me in the face and everything goes bright shocking yellow and hot and my eyes blurry and reeling and I want to cry so I squeeze them shut hoping he'll go away in the darkness disappear in the darkness Gamps disappears but even when I close my eyes it's not black but deep blood colored the same as Iltday beating my eyes throbbing like hearts.

"Nosir" I say. My voice is far away coming from somewhere down deep a smaller version sewed up inside me.

He pops me again in the face. Everything's shaking and stinging and I'm sobbing. I bury my head in my arms and say again "Nosir."

He quits hitting me then yells at me to turn off the d*mned racket. He means Jerry Springer and Rush Limbaugh and Bill Ray Cyrus and me watching *The Wizard of Oz.*

But I can't move and this makes him madder. He calls me a blubbering idiot. Shoves me towards my room. As he does this he teeters and falls and Stan comes loose. The cabinet nearby rattles all those ceramic elf figurines inside shaking and clinking and watching us with rosy cheeks and big bright-blue eyes.

"Gamps!" I yell and help him stand and fit into his leg.

"D*mn strap's loose" he says.

Once he's standing I grab his cane for him and rush into the den and shut off the TV and the radio and my personal recorder then into the kitchen to turn off the boombox except that "Achy Breaky Heart" had already ended and the tape player shut itself off by then. And it's quiet as all heck in here. No more scratching.

Gamps hobbles into the kitchen. Calmer now. Sweating a little bit. Me too. We always sweat in the summers and spring and fall sometimes too. And there was one Christmas years ago when it reached 80 degrees Fahrenheit. Gamps joked that it was a Christmas sweater and though I didn't get what was so funny I laughed and laughed along with him. In All-Star Class Mrs. Kelly taught us that it's all right to laugh at someone's jokes even if you don't understand them because it makes people feel good about themselves.

I help Gamps sit down at the kitchen table.

"Go ahead and put on that Kenny Rogers tape I got there."

I do it. It's *Daytime Friends – The Very Best of Kenny Rogers* by Kenny Rogers. Gamps's tape. Billy Ray Cyrus is mine and then I have the "Electric Boogie" single and a few others like all the audio recordings of *The Wizard of Oz* I recorded with my Azimuth W-2046 Personal Portable Recorder and Cassette Player with Built-In and External Microphone and Stereo System and also a bunch of "Achy Breaky Heart" mixtapes.

When the music kicks in Gamps sighs and puts up his good leg on the adjacent chair.

"Hot dog" he says. "I'm sorry boy. Don't know what came over me. I just... I... it was a strange sensation. Sit down Skeet."

I sit next to him after shifting a broken microwave into the space beneath the table. There aren't but two free chairs in the kitchen. All the others got things piled up on them. Broken toasters and microwaves and boxes of found utensils and food I'm not supposed to eat 'cause it's expired but which it would nonetheless be a shame to waste. Things like that.

"You forgive your old Gamps?"

I nod. "Yessir."

"That's good. You're a good boy. Hardworking boy. Just a bit thick-headed I guess. Little bit muddled."

"Yessir."

"Some strange feeling came over me just then. I can't explain it very well. I don't want you in that attic. I just saw you there and I thought of Gumma God rest her soul and I lost my cool. Ain't fair. Ain't fair what's happened to this famn damily"

"I won't Gamps. I'm sorry Gamps. I'm sorry."

"Forget it. I went out... got groceries."

I slump a little. I like going out to go shopping with Gamps for groceries and etc. at the Willy Nilly's but he is always going without me saying he needs alone time needs Gamps time road time. Time. I don't like the word. A sinking feel in my gut. Time away from me.

"Perk up Skeet. I got fried chicken and biscuits and sweet tea for our repast. Also slaw and taters. A feast for kings yessir. Now hop to it and get the groceries in here and clear us a spot on the table."

So I do and pretty soon we have our dinner though it isn't but four o'clock. Gamps takes his repast earlier in the day than most. Still it feels wrong.

Seems a chunk missing from the day.

Seems I missed something.

It's pretty good food. We eat the whole doggone bucket with the sweet tea and taters (mashed that is with thick brown gravy) slaw and biscuits. The yellow over everything isn't very appetizing but the food tastes good and it gives me enough energy to think up an ending for my story that I had been writing earlier today about me and Deidre Thomas and Gamps. The two of them get in an argument and Gamps pops Deidre Thomas for not listening to him then I come in and tell everyone to just "Cool it!" and Deidre Thomas gives me a hug and Gamps nods and says I was right to say "Cool it!" at him like that and gives me a hard pat on the shoulder and so I say "Cool it!" again and everyone laughs and we drive back home in the Belleville sedan which glitters in the yellow sun.

I tell Gamps the ending of the story and he stares at the greasy bones on his plate and the leftover puddle of slaw. Stares for a real long time without offering any comment on my story and eventually goes back to his bed still wearing his favorite t-shirt which has a whole bunch more on the back actually with pretty cool flames.

When Gumma was around she was a force of cleanliness and getting rid of things. Every Sunday a big clean was her ritual and other days just the tidying and dishes and whatnot. Except for Iltdays. Iltdays have always been an exception. People just jitter mostly in their bones Iltdays glowing that deep red that shines from within.

Then she left us.

I don't know what to make of it. Lord knows. I don't know what to make of it.

Well now it's my turn to clean. It's always my turn. Stan makes it difficult for Gamps to stand by the sink to wash or put dishes away or do any tidying up. And so it falls on old Skeet Jeffcoat. Which I don't mind actually. I got lots going on in my mind when I'm doing the cleaning up. I wipe the paper buckets clean with my rag and nest them inside all our other buckets on the counter. Most of them are stuck together now and got bugs scrambling all over them (but not fire ants—praise Jesus). Cleaning's easy and bugs do most of the work anyhow. Palmetto bugs I mean—and flies. Gamps's a bit scared of palmetto bugs and doesn't like to root around in the kitchen cabinets where I stuff all the paper buckets and styrofoam from takeout because they're crawling with bugs most of the time. But the bugs just eat up all the leftover bits we didn't eat and which I didn't wipe off.

They're my little kitchen helpers.

Then we do some TV and it's some nonsensical art movie on every channel with marble stairs that never seem to want to end and a big iron door at the top that looks too heavy to open and mists lapping against the stairs mists the color of blood. The program lasts for hours it seems and Gamps is snoring in the chair remote dangling off his good hand (that would be his left one—the right is mostly nubs). I could grab it and change the station but I can't take my eyes from the TV show. Frantic breathing as someone's climbing the stairs. And every now and then a shot of that door. You never actually see that the door is at the top of the stairs because the viewer is always climbing.

But.

I guess.

You know it somehow. Somehow you know it'll be there. Waiting.

Then the lights in our room flicker and Gamps snaps awake shouting about his leg and his face is purple the neck cords standing out as if he's in pain and when I turn back to the television I see that *Star Trek: The Next Generation* is on and not that show about the stairs and door and mist. Which if I'm honest I probably have seen before. Probably not the first time I climbed those stairs via boob-tube programming.

Before bed I brush my teeth and sit at the table in my room for a little more. Studying. But I have trouble remembering the ending of the story I came up with 'cause Deidre Thomas isn't out back anymore and it's pretty dark and something is blocking my thoughts some obstruction up there in my mind. I wipe the shaggy hair off my forehead and rub the center of it. The little depression there in my forehead a little bit of a scar curved and white like a crescent moon.

Hurricane Hugo did quite a job on this house let me tell you. A clean jab through the roof.

In the end I just write my name a bunch of times which is okey dokey cause that's studying too.

Chapter 4
Wednesday

No scratching this morning.

Sign it's going to be a fine day. It's early but Deidre Thomas is outside in shorts and a baggy t-shirt with a thin book in her hands. You can just barely glimpse her down the yard between our houses and around the corner at the patio where she smokes and has her coffee.

Maybe Calders. Maybe not.

Wednesday is a good day to read outside because it's sky blue and if you think about what day it is the sky just melts down on top of everything even if it's overcast the blue behind it soaks through and drips all over everyone.

A beautiful day.

It actually doesn't look too hard from here (her book I mean) and she reads it pretty fast. My story today in blue ink is about how I write this long story about as thick as the one Deidre Thomas my neighbor the girl has but then I don't sign my name after I write it and the book is very famous in the *Pinehouse Chronicle* and everyone reads it especially Deidre Thomas who buys eight copies of it so she can read a different copy for each day of the week including Iltdays and one time she stops by and asks me "did you read this great book which is my favorite and I have eight copies of it?" I say "No

I did not read the great book" and Mr. Lingdenberry (that's Russell Lingdenberry's daddy) makes all the employees of Movie Mayhem read the book and calls it "required reading for all employees" but everyone there already read the danged book anyway.

The story goes on like that for a while.

I can't quite think of a proper ending but the pages are so sweaty near the end it's hard to read the words anyway with all the blue overlapping like trying to write on the surface of a lake.

AC isn't working properly.

By the time I'm done Deidre Thomas's gone inside and I hear Happy Value Shopping going in Gamps's room about a Deluxe Cat Tree which Deidre Thomas might like on account of her having a cat a fat ginger one that likes to explore the shelving we got in our backyard shelving we took from the Rhoda's Discount Store that closed down two years ago after Hurricane Allison made a mess of everything. It was around this time when Deidre Thomas's parents died and Gumma too and Ms. Elsworth. And there was someone else too that died back then though I can't remember who it was for the life of me.

Maybe because it's breakfast time.

For Wednesday breakfast we got frozen Waffacombs Now With Superhex Syrup Pockets and Bubba Joe's (Hear That Sizzle) Ultra Thick Cut Bacon and besides that I make Gamps some Calders. Plus I eat my cereal a big heaping bowl of Joye's Marvel-Os and what's interesting about Marvel-Os is that all the sugary puffs are grayish and the marshmallows are different shapes and colors each one for a different day of the week even red stars for Iltdays.

I bring Gamps our breakfast on the tray and have to knock on his door for some time saying I got our breakfast and boy howdy it's getting cold. And your Calders.

"'Best Cup Is *Every* Cup'" Gamps says his voice muffled through the door.

I mouth that part right as Gamps says it. Used to be I would say it aloud when he said it but one day he smacked me upside the head with Stan and told me to "Shut the f*ck up d*mned parrot!" and ever since then I could only mouth those words. Even so I hunch up a little as I do it remembering the painful shock of Titanium Stan walloping my old noggin.

Sure enough he lets me in (he can just lock and unlock the door from the bed with his plastic reaching claw) and his face is all puffed up and his cataracts look all damp and dog-like and he just grunts at me when I ask him about the Deluxe Cat Tree and how our neighbor that girl Deidre Thomas's cat might like it if we had about ten or so of those things in our backyard. "It could be our Cat Complex."

Gamps takes out the other tray but doesn't take to my Cat Complex idea or contribute in any way.

That's okey dokey too.

In the summertime Wednesday is Lawn Day.

Got to water everything. Got to water the lawn ornaments. Got to water the grass and the tangle of bushes in the front yard. Got to water across the fence in the backyard to the old farm now nothing but hard clay where wild shrubs grow. I search around for a hose. We have a lot of them lying all over the danged place like garter snakes 'cause Gamps and I never established a system for hoses a system for keeping them sorted like the pen tips inside my colored pen. I find the newest one bright green and not too leaky and drag it over to the house spigot. We got a few sprinklers for the grass but the things don't work right hard to explain what happens but the water goes every which way every direction you don't want it to so I generally just handle the grass myself walking around with it and getting all the brown spots. We do have some brown spots if you look real close at the lawn and when I moved our shelving a few months ago it was basically just dirt underneath so I moved them back quick before Gamps could see it.

In addition to watering you have to trim the shrubs and we do have some shrubbery to take care of and besides all that there's the mowing for which I got the old reel mower. It's easier to push over the brown spots and not the high thick clumps of green we got popping up sporadically and then we have all the shelving in the back and Gumma's old Novi hatchback which Gamps is about to get around to fixing up to serve as his around-town car. It's a busy lawn is my point and difficult to mow everything so I mostly just push it around for thirty minutes or so and by now it's too danged hot to think much less do anything else so I take shelter indoors.

A package has arrived from Happy Value Shopping and I could not tell you what it contains. Maybe something from yesterday or last week or before that. Back in the haze of memory. I bring it in to Gamps and he tears it open and turns out it's two clock radios. Gamps tells me to stow them in the hall closet without opening the packages in case they're going to appreciate. The spare room is jammed full of packages mostly Happy Value Shopping but also Treasure Cruising finds and it's been this way for some time now ready to burst out and crush whoever opens the door and the hall closet is just as bad but there is room in the back hall wedged behind the washer and dryer a place not many burglars would look.

We eat a pile of sandwiches for lunch Bubba Joe's Only The Baloney with onion powder and mustard and Chee-Zee Paste which is Monday orange even if today is Wednesday and while we eat I put on the Billy Ray Cyrus tape and show off to Gamps my two-stepping and that gets him tapping his foot and laughing. A pretty good time all and all.

Today being Wednesday and our lunch all eaten up it is about time to go on our Treasure Cruise which is about the most exciting thing Gamps and I do together. We pile into the Hamtramck and bump on down Sumter Road that's the road we live on and in case I get lost I need to tell someone my name is Skeet Jeffcoat Deveaux and our address is 512 Sumter Road and our phone number's 803-555-6713.

At the end of Sumter Road we turn onto Sandhills Highway then it's nothing but forest and farmland for a couple of miles. The same way I go when I walk to EAT or Movie Mayhem. The highway passes by the First Baptist Church of Pinehouse which looks like an iceberg exploded out of the ground and rising out of the lawn beside it is a crucifix several stories tall the biggest in the state I'm proud to say.

Gamps takes the turn to West Main which is where the Willy Nilly's is and the Quick Change where Gamps gets the oil changed and their prices are pretty reasonable. Here we pass the famous sign Welcome to Pinehouse Pop. 6305 Real American City 1992! And as we pass by Gamps shouts "Real American City My *ss!" We have a good laugh about this. Then Gamps grows serious and whispers "My *ss." Not so funny the second time so we don't laugh.

Then we cross the bridge over the narrowest part of Pinehouse Lake and right there is EAT where my friend Deidre Thomas works just about every danged day of the week.

Pinehouse is certainly pretty we both do agree about that. They built a Kirby's Drive-In the year we received the Real American City Award. Then there's a Burger Braggers and Commander Clucker and Grease Bros. Pizza. There's also Hudson's Subs and Grub which isn't a chain but it's got pretty good sandwiches and burgers too. There's no Supercity Store but we've got a Slash Spree and that does just fine. Used to be there was Rhoda's Discount Store but Slash Spree pushed them out of business. So says Gamps. Then there's the movie theater and the town hall. On the other end of town is a big old strip mall with a bunch of empty shops but among them a Beau Department Store and Movie Mayhem where I'm proud to work as Video Store Clerk.

Gamps has mapped out the most efficient route for us to take in the Real American City proper and we see just about everything there is to see be it Pinehouse High School where I graduated Class of '95 Staying Alive or the little downtown with the Pinehouse Police Station where I had to go that one time and boy I was really upset and scared but they did give me a bunch of bottles of Atomic Fizz Neon Lime Flavor (Fear the Fizz) and chocolate-frosted custard-filled donuts from Dunno Donuts. Then the park which has got a fountain and a tree and a bench with an old man sitting on it. Then we see houses and lawns and people out in the heat walking their dogs and kids riding their bikes or playing with sprinklers in the yard.

Today we discover some great treasures. There's:

Titani-Man weight bench with a crumpled base

Arctic Trek 1740 folding treadmill with a ripped-up tread (pulled from the same house as the Titani-Man)

bent curtain rod

wooden chair with loose leg (which Gamps says he can fix up easy enough)

stained twin bed mattress next to a dismantled bed (good for Bounce House I reckon)

toilet in fine condition

assortment of terracotta flowerpots

two birdcages with bird smell but no birds

laundry basket with snapped rim

mannequin torso and arms

Azimuth 19-inch television with spiderwebbed screen

warped and water-stained end table

That's the big stuff. We don't go rooting around in garbage bags much anymore not since the police stopped us last year and gave Gamps a warning but I do peek in from time to time at what all is lying on top.

Late in the day the scratching starts up again and the strange thing about the scratching is I can hear it even when I go out back and unload some of our stuff and arrange it around the yard. Somehow it's both outside and in the attic too.

A very tricky kind of scratching.

Gamps has poker at the American Legion on Wednesday nights leaving me to fend for myself. Think I'll go to EAT and say hi to my neighbor and friend the girl Deidre Thomas. Truth is I need to go out 'cause of the doggone scratching. It's begun to smell a bit too if I'm honest with you Ma'am. Gamps said he would handle it but since he hasn't yet I ought to just get on the heck out of here. Used to be that Gumma would get all this business handled 'cause she didn't want Gamps paining himself what with Stan and all and I reckon I could handle it too but Gamps has his own thoughts on that subject.

I had a dream once that our attic was actually a proper second floor and the ceiling of the hallway was very tall and spacious and instead of the pull down there was a set of stairs much wider than the hallway with fingers of red mist curling down them and they led up to an iron door with a funny shape. Uneven and kind of like a honeycomb or rather made up of thousands of tiny honeycombs a bit like Waffacombs and their Superhex Syrup Pockets actually. It was cold and dark and you could feel it was very thick and heavy when you opened it but once you opened it there was nothing inside. The door just kept opening and the wind whipped around you and the cold rushed in and then the dream was over. I think it was a dream or maybe something on the boob tube I saw. But ever since then sometimes when I enter the hallway I'm a little surprised at the height of the ceiling and I'm a little surprised by the pull down and I think about that biting cold and I'm happy it's as hot as it is and that our AC is so fickle. Still I may peek over my shoulder or look through a mirror into the hallway to see if it changed back again but it never does.

I brush my teeth and put on my combat boots and a fresh pair of jean shorts and a white polo. Comb my hair and brush my teeth and look pretty danged respectable.

Everyone on Sumter Road has their bins out as well as miscellaneous items that Gamps and I might have missed on our Treasure Cruise earlier today. So when I head out for dinner I take a meandering route crossing back and forth and checking out what all everyone's throwing away. I didn't put out our own bin because this week there wasn't much refuse. I do try to reuse and save as much as possible.

Across the street is an ironing board with a scorch mark and ripped fabric cover that I heft up and bring back home setting it on the small front porch which is packed full of other interesting items mostly taken from across the street.

Next door Deidre Thomas doesn't have any miscellaneous bits but she is recycling an awful lot of wine bottles and beer cans. Even though we both graduated together in '95 Staying Alive I'm actually a year older (I did the math) and I'm the legal drinking age but Deidre Thomas is not so I don't know how she keeps getting all this stuff. Maybe her parents had a bunch of beer and wine refrigerators fully stocked before they were murdered. She's probably got a room in her house filled to the brim with alcohol refrigerators that's gotta be it. Though I can buy Gamps his Brewster now I can't drink it because I don't have the brain cells to spare. So says Gamps anyway. Gumma always said alcohol was for people who want to forget things and sometimes it's hard enough for me to remember everything important so I figure I'm not missing much.

I open up her trash bin and it smells like eggshells and coffee grounds. I scrounge around a bit then see a blue moon glinting from the insert inside a plastic cassette tape case. I pull it out and scratch off some of the dried egg and wipe off the coffee grounds which stained the insert a little. It's an Aurimax 60-minute which is 30 on each side. A mixtape actually. The track listing is:

Side A

1. Billy Ray Cyrus – "Achy Breaky Heart" (last minute)

2. Billy Ray Cyrus – "Achy Breaky Heart" (first minute)

3. Billy Ray Cyrus – "Achy Breaky Heart" (whole thing except a bit in the middle)

Side B

1. Billy Ray Cyrus – "Achy Breaky Heart" (whole thing but a few seconds at the start)

2. Billy Ray Cyrus – "Achy Breaky Heart" (minute here or there)

3. Billy Ray Cyrus – "Achy Breaky Heart" (last minute)

4. Billy Ray Cyrus – "Achy Breaky Heart" (whole thing very nearly)

5. Billy Ray Cyrus – "Achy Breaky Heart" (first few seconds)

6. Billy Ray Cyrus – "Achy Breaky Heart" (middle bit)

It doesn't mention all the silences between the song fragments and these are good because they help build up the suspense and the final surprise when the music cuts in. My coworker Russell Lingdenberry taught me all about mixtapes and how you're supposed to make them for girls you… well he said something dirty but I think what he meant was when you like a girl. I was going to draw a heart on the cover but actually my favorite Marvel-O shape is blue moons and not pink hearts because blue is my favorite color because it is the color of happiness and also the color of Wednesday which is my favorite day of the week so as you can see there are many reasons for it to be a blue moon on the cover and not a heart pink or otherwise. A blue heart might have worked too but there're no blue heart in a box of Joye's Marvel-Os.

I clean up the cassette tape and put it in her mailbox.

Across the street from Deidre Thomas's house is a cabinet of plastic drawers that are cracked so you couldn't store liquid in them but you could probably put VHS tapes or construction paper or envelopes or other non-liquid items inside them so I reckon Gamps would call this a find. Several houses down is a bicycle with no front wheel. I also manage to pick up old copies of the *Pinehouse Chronicle* and *The Magnolia*.

At the end of Sumter Road I turn onto the highway and walk on the shoulder a tight one this shoulder where there's just a bit of room between the overgrown grass where you're likely as not to get a tick bite and the road with a 55 mph speed limit. It's a pretty dangerous walk I'd say but I can't drive the golf cart out here on account of it being so slow. Tried it once and let me tell you there was a big to-do.

Cars whiz past every now and again and raise up a hot wind some of them honking at me and I wave and holler back smiling my Pinehouse High School Class of '95 Staying Alive Best Smile. An eighteen-wheeler roars by and I'm about knocked off my danged feet in the vortex of dirt and grit in its wake.

It's a long walk past pine woods. Planted woods. Alleys of trees. You see other trees in Pinehouse I suppose—magnolias or oaks or dogwoods—but the general impression you get is of pine every inch of the town sprouting pine like these giant hundred-foot-tall weeds. If you don't mow as well as I do you get pine saplings in the yard tender flexible things branches like matchsticks and needles like hair soft downy hair and if you were to become incapacitated and were stuck at home staring out at the yard you'd have a problem on your hands yes Ma'am better believe it a forest sprouting up in the blink of an eye.

You'd be swallowed up by pine weeds.

The pine forest becomes broken and sparse. Across the road is a farm stretching forever with cows grazing in a field in the distance tiny as little white-and-brown toys. Then there's the First Baptist Church of Pinehouse which I may have already told you about and a host of ranch houses with well-manicured lawns and here the sidewalk begins which means I made it safe. Once again.

Soon enough I'm passing by the Welcome to Pinehouse Pop. 6305 Real American City 1992! "Real American City My *ss" I whisper since Gamps isn't here to say it. I don't actually say the curse word of course. Gumma taught me better than that. Taught me not to use cuss words and not to kill insects and to always say yessir or yes ma'am and to always open doors for the fairer sex and to give everything your Skeet Jeffcoat Deveaux best.

In bright red letters set against the Wednesday-blue sunset sky the sign for EAT rises up about fifty feet off the ground nearly as high as the First Baptist crucifix I'd wager. A car honks at me as it drives by and someone shouts out my name. Halfway across the bridge over Pinehouse Lake you can see into the restaurant can see Deidre Thomas the girl and my neighbor at the counter and the cook Jim Byrd who was Pinehouse High School Class of '93 and I don't know what their slogan was or if it rhymed with '95 the way ours did. The car that honked at me has pulled into the parking lot and I see that there's three people from my class in the diner now and sitting down to eat.

I enter and stand there and stare over the counter at Jim Byrd who is smoking a cigarette and greets me with a nod and a half-smile on his face. A half-smile like a half-moon. "Look for moons today." That ought to have been my daily meditation but actually I forgot to read the meditation this morning.

Jim is big like me. He played tennis I think 'cause I remember he always walked around the halls of Pinehouse High School with a tennis racket strapped to his backpack and then he got into a car crash and has all these scars on his legs now and smokes and works at EAT and I don't see the tennis racket anymore with him.

"Go ahead and have a seat Skeet. Anywhere you like." It's Deidre's voice. It makes me feel warm and pleasant inside but also strangely frozen and transfixed. Deidre Thomas the girl my neighbor and great friend. As you may have noticed she doesn't need to call me Skeet Jeffcoat Deveaux my full name. Or Sir or Mr. Deveaux. She's still taking orders at the table of my classmates. Our classmates actually. We all went to Pinehouse High School. It's a kind of reunion I guess. Am I supposed to make a speech about that or what? I was voted Best Smile in my class after all.

They're all sitting at the rear of the restaurant in one of the booths of blue-and-white-striped leather and right by them is a window overlooking the lake. I pick a booth on the lakeside too a couple down from them so we can chat if we want. The water through the glass behind them is dark but still reflecting in rippling stripes the blue fires of Wednesday's sunset.

I pick up a menu from the holder at the end of the table and pretend to look through it while I secretly watch Deidre Thomas over the top. She's already finished with them and by them I mean the customers who are the only other customers in the restaurant and after she hands the ticket to Jim she comes over to me and I move my eyes down onto the menu where the words dance around making them impossible to read then I look down at her red-and-white sneakers standing out against the checkered tiles.

"Hi Skeet. How's it going?"

I clear my throat.

"Can I get you something?"

I swallow and look back up at the menu.

She waits for me to answer and I really can't think of anything to say and I don't dare look over at her she's too close and I can't remember why I came here.

"You want something to eat or not?" She waits. "You have to speak to me Skeet if you want service."

"Yes Ma'am" I say. My throat feels thick and dry and sticky all at once. I turn towards her and look down again at her red-and-white sneakers.

She laughs a short laugh. A chuckle I guess you'd call it. Not as enthusiastic as mine. "Okay. What'll it be?"

"P-pancakes."

"All right."

"With the. B-b-butter on top. Of it."

"Gotcha."

"And sausages."

"Links or patties?"

"Patties. I guess. Are those Bubba Joe's Original Breakfast Sausage Patties Taste That Country Kitchen?"

She laughs again. Deidre has an interesting laugh kind of dry like a cough and always coming when something isn't all that funny. "Gee. I'm not sure. You want me to check for you?"

I can't think what to say.

"Skeet...? Skeet...? How about something to drink?"

"I reckon... sweet tea... iced tea."

"Can do."

"Thank you. Ma'am."

"No problemo Skeet."

She leaves and my body relaxes 'cause it had tensed up a bit when I forgot all about why I had come to EAT in the first place which is funny if you think about it since the place is called EAT and all. I put the menu back in the holder and start laughing a little about what just happened.

"Skeet Jeffcoat Deveaux!" someone shouts out.

Another one says "Don't call him. He'll come over."

A couple of them start laughing. Snickering you might call it.

I get up and walk over. "Hi y'all" I say.

There's three of them which I may have mentioned and I don't remember their names except for Tom Porter 'cause he and I used to be friends way back when. This was before I lived on Sumter Road before Deidre Thomas was my neighbor. Magnolia Avenue. A different house than mine and Gamps's. Next door to the Porter family house. One time last year after we picked up some Commander Clucker fried chicken Gamps drove us by this house from long ago and we stopped across the road and he looked at it for some time without saying anything. Then he turned to me and asked if I remembered this house. A white house with a blue door and two windows with the blinds pulled. And there were some baby toys scattered about the yard not mine I guess but some other kid's.

"Heck I don't remember a darned thing about it. That's what I told Gamps" I say thinking back on that time in the truck with Gamps.

The girl and guy I don't know start laughing and Tom is looking at me funny 'cause I must have just said that out loud and I get the sense that they had been talking to me or maybe about me. Of course they were. After all I'm standing right in front of them.

"You'n Tom's old buddies ain't that right Skeet?"

The guy I don't know says this. He smells like Gamps does after he smoked and drank too much the previous day. He looks familiar but he was not Best Smile or Most Talented or Most Likely to Be Successful or Most Athletic and he wasn't a friend of mine so I can't tell you who he is. And the girl is wearing a Pinehouse High School letter jacket which has a blue-and-white wasp on it like that blue-and-white house on Magnolia Avenue and the blue-and-white décor of the restaurant EAT and the blue and white of writing a story on Wednesday and the girl has long red hair but I don't reckon I know her either.

"Tom and I're good buddies." I confirm this because that must be why they called me over here. Just to straighten matters up.

The diner is quiet so you can hear the rap music from Jim Byrd's radio and the food sizzling on the skillet and it smells like hamburger cooking up. Makes my stomach rumble.

"Before they fixed you up right?" The guy winks at me and I don't know if it's a good kind of wink or another kind of wink.

"Greg shut up dude" Tom says.

"They fixed me up all right" I say.

The guy I don't know laughs. "They turned you into a parrot didn't they?"

I laugh at this too. "Parrot." I laugh again.

The girl I don't know her face has gone redder than her hair and she's trying to hide it from me. Her fingernails are painted bright pink which in case you didn't know is the color of Friday and not today. A little mix-up is all it is these colors on mismatching days.

"Hey Skeet." The guy I don't know gestures for me to get closer. "Can you show it to me?"

"Quit it Greg" Tom says.

I lean in close and say "I don't know what you're talking about Guy I Don't Know."

Shaking his head he stifles more laughter. "The scar. On your head. I heard it was behind your bangs. That's why you keep your hair shaggy. Ain't it?"

"Skeet your sweet tea's here!" It's Deidre Thomas's voice. I straighten up and see her standing by my table one hand on her hip. She looks madder than heck oh boy what did I do wrong now?

"Yes Ma'am." I go over there and squeeze into the booth without making eye contact with her. Dang it I wasn't trying to get Deidre Thomas mad at me.

Guy I Don't Know does something weird with his voice and he sounds a little robotic when he talks. "Yes Ma'am."

Deidre Thomas walks over to them. "Y'all are gonna have to leave."

Tom Porter starts to stand.

"The h*ll we are" Guy I Don't Know says firmly planted in his seat.

"Out of here. Now."

"Where's our food Most Talented Waitress?"

"It's burnt" Jim Byrd says. He's walked around the counter and is soon standing by Deidre Thomas. He's about a head taller than she is. "And inedible."

"And y'all ain't serving me why? Because I was having a bit of fun with Skeet Jeffcoat Deveaux?" Guy I Don't Know turns around in the booth which squeaks mightily and I lower my head and drink my sweet tea. "Skeet Jeffcoat Deveaux! You and me's buddies right? We was just having a laugh. Ain't it so?"

I don't answer. I'm not. Sure. What is the answer.

Jim Byrd leans down over the table and says something in a low voice I don't hear and sure enough it seems Tom Porter and his friends turned out not to be too hungry after all 'cause they skedaddle.

"Want a burger for your dinner Dee?" Jim Byrd asks the girl my neighbor Deidre Thomas.

She chuckles that dry chuckle.

My pancakes come out just as expected with a side of sausage patties and a ball of butter on top.

Jim Byrd and Deidre Thomas chat while I eat and they smoke at the counter drinking coffee like Gamps does. When Jim steps out back Deidre comes around with more tea and after she pours it she slides into the booth across the table from me. And for the longest time she just sits there and doesn't do or say anything. I keep taking small sips of sweet tea even though I don't feel like I could drink another drop like it's just filling up in the back of my throat. I catch a glimpse of her Thursday-green eyes then look down at the puddle of syrup and pancake and sausage crumbs.

"Sorry about them Skeet. Sorry about those *ssholes."

I don't know what she's apologizing to me for. I feel like it should be me apologizing. I take another sip of tea.

"Skeet?" she says. "Skeet can I ask you something?"

I nod. "Yes Ma'am."

"It's been two years now since you lost your grandma hasn't it?"

I nod. "Yes Ma'am."

"For me too. Two years since I lost my parents."

I nod. "Yes Ma'am."

"Do you know? What happened?"

I shake my head. "No Ma'am."

"You don't need to call me Ma'am Skeet. We're practically the same danged age."

"Yes. Ma'am." I try not to say Ma'am but can't help it.

Her hand reaches across the table and squeezes mine. I stare at it without daring to move. "Do you remember what happened that night? Because I saw you. Did you know that? I was out at a movie with Sterling Dixon. Remember him? He drove me home that night. My parents didn't really approve of him so he dropped me off right at the neighborhood entrance and I walked the rest of the way. And as I was walking up... I saw you. Saw you running out of my house. Then you... vanished. There one second. Gone the next. It was me you know. Me that told the police you'd been in my house." She pauses. "Do you understand any of this? Do you understand what I'm saying to you?"

I nod.

"I'm the reason y'all were arrested. I'm sorry. I know you're harmless. Know you wouldn't hurt a fly." That's true. Gumma taught me better than that. "Guess it doesn't matter now though." Another pause. A long one. "Skeet please tell me. I need to know. Back then. I thought it must have been you. But when I think back on it I realize you were chasing after someone. Chasing and hollering after whoever it was that murdered my parents. I thought about leaving. About going down to Florida or I don't know—"

She stops abruptly. Her hand withdraws. Jim Byrd has stepped back inside and he looks over at us before disappearing back into the store room or whatever it is back beyond the door in the kitchen.

Deidre Thomas turns back to me and I look down at the remains of my dinner.

"But I can't. I'm stuck. Here. I'm stuck here. I can't bring myself to leave. I need to know what happened. And you're the only one that can tell me. Skeet please. Please."

I think about it some. Think back on the night Gumma died but there's nothing there. Like the dream of stairs. It's like the words scribbled out in a story you write in your Skoolbrite Notebook in Tuesday yellow. You see the impression of it and the evidence that it's been scratched out and you can almost make out the letters but really it's just a confusion just a mess just scratching just scratching just scratching—

Scratch scratch scratch.

"Please" I say looking up at her and kind of fall forward into the pools of color of her eyes. The deep seas of pine of Pinehouse Real American City! edged with the blue of today. "Please."

"Please what?" Deidre asks. The light in her eyes shifts. "Are you mimicking me? No. No. You're not are you?"

"Please."

Scratch scratch scratch.

"The door is opening" I say.

"What?"

"Iltday is coming."

"Ilt... day?"

"Yes Ma'am."

"Skeet? You've gone... pale. Are you okay?" Her voice is tiny and everything but her eyes has darkened and deformed pulled away from me like long pulls of taffy like they had in Charleston when Gamps and Gumma and I went except those were all pastel colors and these are the blue of Wednesday and the deep green of her eyes a pine forest underwater—

"Skeet?"

—and currents ripping through the branches bending like grass and the stirring shadows.

The scratching starts up again but now I realize it's not coming from the attic. No. I was wrong about that. Hot dang I was wrong. There never was any scratching in the attic. It was inside all along.

Inside my head.

My scalp is tingling and there's a horrible pressure like I'm the heart of an exploding mine that blows off legs and fingers and leaves a man crippled and bitter and the scratching is so loud I can't hear anything else it's legs it's insect or crab or human legs poking out of my head and into my ears frantic like scattering cockroaches.

And then I remember Deidre Thomas the girl my best friend and neighbor's eyes staring at me from across the table and all the swimming images grow still and all kinds of color ray out and fill in the dark the shadow the world.

I remember myself and look back down at my plate.

Syrup.

Crumbs.

"Skeet?"

"Yes Ma'am" I say. I'm out of breath. Haven't even done any running around and I'm all out of breath.

"Skeet you okay?"

I nod. "I reckon so. Yes Ma'am."

Chapter 5
Thursday

Thursday is interesting for the green of it. Pine green. Darker than other greens so dark sometimes that when you look at a pine tree on Thursday it gets so dark green it's practically black.

Thursday's also a showering day. It's a bit complicated because our shower stall doubles as storage and you can imagine all the things we get stacked up in there. AC window units and paint cans and whatnot. But I move things around till the stall accommodates me and get it going.

Next is breakfast. I make waffles and bacon with plenty of syrup and butter and bring them to Gamps's room.

—*Please*—

He's watching the weather. There's a wall-sized weather map with the Gulf Coast covered in a giant white whorl and dotted lines curving up the Atlantic Coast towards us from the looks of it. Right towards the Palmetto State.

They're calling it Danny.

A Category 1. Not too terribly bad. The worst is Category 5 and I lived through one of those which was called Hugo back when I was thirteen. That was scary. I hid in the bathtub with a bunch of pillows and the whole house shuddered like something with giant claws was rattling us and the pine tree stabbed through our roof. Gumma said I had been brave even though I'd only been hiding.

"Might veer off they say. Could hit though." No Happy Value Shopping this morning with the talk of the hurricane absorbing Gamps's attention.

Once we're finished eating he roots around in the pocket of his jeans hanging on the bed post.

"Take a looky here." He tosses down fifty or so one-dollar bills loose and wrinkled and creased and dogeared things nicked and hassled with a strong oily smell. "Raked it in last night at the American Legion."

"Hot dog Gamps."

"You d*mn right hot dog." He rubs his thick beard. "Took those old boys to school."

I give a big laugh and he joins in. I do love that sound. As much as I used to love hearing the sounds of Deidre Thomas practicing the piano next door playing the same loop of notes over and over for hours.

"Tell you what. Get that there boombox and the Kenny Rogers tape."

"Today's Thursday Gamps" I say getting out of the bed.

"That's right." He sniffs. "What time is it anywho?"

"It's 9:30 Gamps" I say after checking my Chronometrix Radio-Glo Watch.

"H*ll you gonna be late." He shovels in the last of his waffle and bacon while I wait there watching him. "Help me up you bipedal idiot. We'll do Kenny on the road."

By the time we arrive at Movie Mayhem Stan is itching like crazy.

"I need a danged hot bath" Gamps says. He's sweating from the itchiness. Interesting to think a fake leg can itch like that but it's the Christ-forsaken truth I tell you.

Watching him scratch at the loose fabric around his metal leg reminds me of something. "Oh yeah. Hey Gamps. Seems like that scratching went away. Didn't it?"

He stops scratching and looks over at me. "Guess so. Saves me a trip up the pull down. Hope nothing died. Welp. Pick us out something funny to watch for a change there Skeet. No more d*mn musicals."

"All right sir."

"Get going then."

"All right sir. Bye Gamps."

He grunts.

Russell Lingdenberry is inside waiting for me.

"Well howdy-f*cking-do pardner."

I nod. "Morning Russell."

He is my Pinehouse High School Class of '95 Staying Alive classmate along with Deidre Thomas and we're pretty good friends in addition to coworkers. He has his picture a couple of pages after mine on page 43 in the yearbook but we weren't in the same class 'cause he was not in Mrs. Kelly's All-Star Class with me. My neighbor Deidre Thomas has her picture several pages later which is pretty interesting and also convenient 'cause if you fold the pages just right or cut out the pictures like I did you can line the three of us up and we look like quite a team.

"That has got to be the gayest d*mn belt I ever did see." He's talking about my belt. Couldn't find my normal one so I'm trying out this new one I found a cowboy's with a longhorn buckle and covered in rhinestones.

"It's pretty sick" I say. That's what Russell says when something's cool. It's totally sick or it's f*cking sick. But he also says that when he's not feeling well and won't be coming in to work or when something grosses him out so generally it's a safe word to use all the danged time.

"You're sick is more like it."

"I. Am. Sick." I nod along to each word like there's music like I'm rocking out. That's how Russell listens to music. I've seen him do it in his car when he didn't think anyone was there. But I was there. I was watching him.

He laughs. Russell's tall and skinny with frameless glasses that are always catching the light and long greasy hair that he only washes once every other week because chicks dig the smell of the natural oils.

"Saunter on out there and empty the bin after you clock in Angel Eyes."

"All right Russell."

I go into the back office and punch the clock then get the keys and head outside to collect the returns in the drive-by box which is detached from the store right on the edge of the sidewalk. I cart them back in and run the tapes through the Lumovox 1-Way VHS Rewinder. It's pretty quick at rewinding. The thing whirs and vibrates when you pop in the tape and has this pleasant ozone smell as the tape heats up from the speed of it. Russell complains about this part of the job but I like it 'cause you get to sit down and just look at the art on the movie covers. *Phantasm* and *Pulp Fiction* and *Indecent Proposal. Under Siege. Something About Mary.* "A raunchy raucous comedy!" the box says. Gamps might like this one.

Russell comes around to my side of the counter and watches me rewinding the tapes. He's wearing a Marilyn Manson t-shirt which I don't like looking at me with its milky eyes 'cause well you can see the black veins standing out on his face. You look at that face and you think about all the people you know that have died. So I look down instead at his black cross trainers.

"I tell you what. We're going to be getting in DVDs soon. You heard of them? Like a CD movie. We've already got a player at my house. And you know what that means don't you? No more f*cking rewinding. Thank God."

"I like rewinding."

"Well you won't be doing it anymore. DVDs you just pop them back on the shelf with no hassle about it. All these tapes we'll trash them eventually."

I don't like that. I don't like what he's saying. I don't like the way he's talking to me. I don't like his Marilyn Manson t-shirt. I don't know what I'd do if there wasn't this Lumovox 1-Way VHS Rewinder to fill in my time at work. Wouldn't feel right coming in and not giving the tapes a good inspection and run through and listening to the whir of it feeling the vibration and the heated smell of the tape.

"You don't trash these tapes. You give them to me and Gamps. We'll open our own store called Skeet and Gamps's VHS No DVD."

Russell wanders back out to the aisles. To the horror section I guess to find something to put on. He always goes there early in the morning when there aren't hardly any customers in the store. When he comes back he puts a tape on and soon all the televisions look like they're dripping with greenish blood and women are screaming everywhen their lips not synced up with their voices then knives flash and eyeballs pop bones cracking through rubbery flesh teeth scattering across concrete no end to it no end.

"I don't like this movie" I say loudly and wipe the sweat off my brow. I think about that scratching at home for some reason. That *scratch scratch scratch*ing. Maybe it came back while I was at work. Come to think of it it seems I had learned something about the scratching last night. Something important. But I can't think now what that might be.

"That's 'cause you're a pussy. This is Lucio Fulci. Serious cinema. Not your lame-*ss musicals." Don't know if I ought to bleep out pussy or not. Guessing not since you can say pussy cat and it's fine not gonna raise any eyebrows.

Doesn't take me too long to finish the rewinding.

No hassle really.

I collect the movies and wheel the bin around the store and put them back on the shelves which is pretty complicated actually the most complicated aspect of my job. We got New Releases and Drama and Comedy and Action/Adventure and Horror and Science Fiction and Foreign and Kids and Musicals and Documentaries and Video Games. I like Musicals a lot. Did I mention that? I've seen all of them about a million times each. The best hands down being *The Wizard of Oz* and if you haven't seen that well I'm just sorry for you Ma'am. I haven't seen the whole thing on account of the angry trees and the nasty old green-faced witch and the flying monkeys parts I just can't bring myself to watch and so shut my eyes and hum

"Ding-dong! The Witch Is Dead" with my fingers plugging up my ears which you can hear if you listen to one of my audio recordings of me watching the movie that I made with my Azimuth W-2046 Personal Portable Recorder and Cassette Player with Built-In and External Microphone and Stereo System. But the scary parts end eventually and I can watch Dorothy and Toto and the Scarecrow and the Tin Man and the Cowardly Lion on their fun adventure. I guess what I like best about it is that Dorothy makes all these special friends and they help her out and everyone sticks together to overcome their challenges. But then Dorothy leaves them. I don't like that part. Why would she leave them alone like that when they had been such a fun and happy family? I hate Dorothy sometimes when I think about it. It's not much of a happy ending. She returns to that Sunday-gray world. No color. Not like in Oz where things are much more interesting even if it is a bit scary sometimes. They have yellow roads in Oz and we only have the boring old blacktop. Not much to look at. Hot dang that's a good movie bringing you such classic songs as "If I Only Had A Brain" and "Follow The Yellow Brick Road" and "Somewhere Over The Rainbow" and many more. The store's copy is a bit wobbly and jumpy by now I watched it so danged much and rewound it and fast-forwarded it to the good parts but Mr. Lingdenberry doesn't know that 'cause no one else hardly rents it 'cause according to Russell it's always airing on TV.

While I shelve the tapes Russell follows me around and talks about all these girls that I don't know. "Let me tell you Skeet. That fine piece of *ss Molly beeped me middle of last night and she wanted it bad and I was like don't be beeping me so late I'll give it to you girl but you gotta be more discreet 'cause I got things going on you know what I mean I could have a girl over here and we could be bumping uglies and she was like I want you so bad Russell I need it so bad."

Pretty boring stuff when Russell opens his mouth and I don't know what he's talking about half the danged time anyway but I listen and nod and go through the movies on the cart and pop them on the shelf. You got to be good with your ABCs got to keep things alphabetized to do this kind of job which is why Mr. Lingdenberry hired me to work at Movie Mayhem because I'm good with my ABCs and I guess Russell isn't so good with them 'cause I have never seen him shelve a video in his life.

Some middle school kids come in carrying skateboards and backpacks and Russell heads to the counter and chats them up. He's always chatting up customers.

"What you delinquents returning?" he asks. "*Dolly Dearest*? H*ll that's child's play. Get it?" The kids laugh hesitantly though I don't understand what the heck is so funny. "Let me help you out. You seen *Night of the Demons*? You girls are gonna piss yourselves." I don't think they're girls either but one's got long hair so it's an easy enough mistake to make.

When the kids leave Russell wanders back over an unlit cigarette dangling from his lips.

"Going out back for a smoke. Beep me if the old man shows up." Russell's got a beeper in case you were wondering a Go-To B280 Numeric Pager. Not that big of a deal actually but he's always fiddling with it. "And if he calls just say I'm in the middle of dropping a deuce."

"All right Russell."

"Repeat it back."

"What?"

"What I just said to you dipsh*t. What you'll say if my dad calls."

I clear my throat and get my phone voice ready. "I'll say 'Hi thank you for calling Movie Mayhem this is Skeet Jeffcoat Deveaux Russell's in the middle of dropping a deuce.'"

Russell grins. "That's my man."

He fist-bumps me.

Sometimes Russell's not so bad.

At lunchtime I get to eat at Burger Braggers. It's pretty close by across the expanse of the parking lot from Movie Mayhem and pretty cheap too. The parking lot used to have a lot of other businesses arranged like a little town all the lots divided by concrete barriers but now there's just Beau Department Store and Movie Mayhem and Burger Braggers and a few empty stores and a few demolished ones which are just concrete slabs with pipes and such sticking out of them and the crumbling remains of walls. I can't remember what happened. A flood maybe or could have been Hugo but I do remember when I was a kid this complex was hopping with activity.

I get three Double-Braggers with Cheese please fries and a Bragger-sized Atomic Fizz Neon Lime Flavor (Fear the Fizz) then take it on back to work.

After lunch a lady drives up and drops a movie into the bin.

"Go out and empty the bin" Russell says after she drives off.

"All right." I do it but not because Russell tells me to not because he's my boss or anything like that. Just because I like to stay on top of things here. There's just the one movie the lady dropped in. *Blue Velvet*. Haven't seen it before. Anyway looks like something I wouldn't want to watch like one of those late-night movies like one of those movies Gamps says you shouldn't watch that kinda thing. I take it back to the Lumovox 1-Way VHS Rewinder and while I'm rewinding it the bell dings.

It's Jim Byrd come to rent a movie.

I may have mentioned to you that he works at EAT and plays tennis and all that but maybe you didn't know that he is a movie buff like me and every day off he has he comes in wearing his wife-beater and gym shorts and tells me about the last movie he watched and that I should watch it if I have the time. Because I'm always looking down at his sandals I notice the scars in his legs long white things with circles next to them like someone missed dotting their i's.

"It's called *The Conversation*" he says. "Gene Hackman. Harrison Ford. Gene Hackman stars as this surveillance expert a loner who plays saxophone along to jazz records during his time off." Deidre Thomas plays saxophone in case I forgot to mention it so I'm already interested in this movie. "The soundtrack alone is phenomenal."

"I like Harrison Ford" I say. "Hey Russell what's Harrison Ford say in that movie?"

"Which movie?"

"That one where they think he killed his wife but he didn't really kill his wife."

Russell thinks hard about this. "Umm let me think."

"You know. It was all some big misunderstanding about his wife getting killed and he said… well I can't remember exactly."

Russell starts giggling. "Man that's a tough one. I can't remember."

Jim Byrd's not laughing. He frowns in fact and mumbles something and looks down at the cart of all the tapes I'm shelving and sees the movie the late-night one I was talking about that *Blue Velvet* movie and asks if he could take it off my hands.

"Well it's a Thursday" I say. "But I guess it's all the same to me if you want to watch a blue movie."

I stare at *The Conversation* cover for a long time after Jim Byrd leaves. Russell's talking in the background I think but I can't really hear what he's saying to me. It's like a syrup around me his voice is passing through it and landing thick in my ears splashing in slow motion not connecting right.

I go over to the player behind the counter and turn off Russell's horror movie.

Russell shouts out from the back office. "Hey *sshole what gives?"

"I'm fixing to watch something" I say.

"Like h*ll you are. Don't get outta line with me Skeet boy."

I pop in the cassette and turn it on.

"It's rumble time." Russell comes out of the office and in a flash the wind explodes out of me and I'm lying on my back and looking up at Russell who's got one knee on my chest and pushing up into my throat.

I gag and struggle against his leg and slap at him. "Let up you sorry old d*ckhead!" I cuss and Ma'am I am deeply sorry about it.

"Like h*ll I will."

"Let up or I'm telling your daddy."

"Like h*ll you will."

"Let up you… you sorry old b*stard."

"B*stard? I'm no f*cking b*stard. You understand what a b*stard is don't you Skeet boy? A b*stard is someone that doesn't know his father. That's you. That's a b*stard. A proper b*stard." He grins about the meanest grin I've ever seen and I pop him in the mouth and I'm truly sorry for it.

Russell rolls off me cussing. "Sh*t. I'm bleeding!" he says. He stares at me with his stupid face and his lips and gums all red as Iltday and his teeth Friday pink. "Touched a nerve did I? F*ck."

"I'm no b*stard. It's not true. I got Gamps."

"He's your grandfather you moron."

"Maybe he's my father too."

Russell laughs touching his mouth tenderly. Blood bubbles between his teeth. "You don't know what the h*ll you're talking about. You don't know how wrong that sounds."

"I'm going home."

"You got three more hours of work left before second shift."

"I don't care. You're being mean to me."

"Mean? *You* punched *me*!"

"Well you started it."

Russell shakes his head. "I was just f*cking around with you anyway. Put your boring turd of a movie on and quit your b*tching. I think we got an ice pack in the fridge in the back office." He heads into the back muttering "Hot-tempered prick."

"I hear you cussing after me" I say.

"Well hear this!" he shouts from the back. "The silent sound of me flipping you the bird."

Filthy. Filthy. I can't stand him sometimes.

That's pretty much how work goes. Russell lets me put on *The Conversation.* For a little while at least. Gene Hackman is an expert at tape recording which I'm also an expert at but Gene Hackman doesn't use an Azimuth W-2046 Personal Portable Recorder and Cassette Player with Built-In and External Microphone and Stereo System like I do. In fact I can't tell what brand he's using. The best bits are when he plays the saxophone. Reminds me of how it used to sound living next to Deidre Thomas. Before she lost her parents. In the movie a powerful politician or someone like that hires Gene Hackman for his tape-recording expertise. This spurs Russell to make a comment muffled by the ice pack against his lip. "Don't know if I told you but Dad's running for mayor in the upcoming election. That's gonna be him there. We gonna be running Pinehouse soon enough."

"Well heck I'd vote for Mr. Lingdenberry." And I would too. He's a kind man smiling and well dressed and never cusses nor says a bad word against me or Gamps.

"I know. That's what I'm saying. He's a shoo-in."

He grows bored and eventually ejects the tape and inserts another horrorfest. Pretty tedious 'cause in addition to being so scary you can't watch half of it the same thing is always happening in all his danged movies which is to say about ten minutes are okay and then a monster or killer appears and it goes downhill with breasts popping out of the television and blood dripping onto the floor.

After Gamps picks me up we swing by the hardware store and I poke through the dumpster nestled out back near the train tracks but there's nothing much good there today. Then we drive home by way of Pinehouse High School where I graduated Class of '95 Staying Alive.

As we're driving I see a sign staked into the roadside that says "Lingdenberry for Mayor – By His Bootstraps" and I say "Hey Gamps what's that sign mean about his bootstraps?"

Because of his cataracts Gamps usually doesn't notice things like this but he just catches sight of it as it blurs past then he brakes and reverses pulling in close and squinting and leaning out the window and he studies the sign with the engine idling. Studies it for a long time. I must've read it about fifteen times before he finally snorts.

"Mr. Lingdenberry's running for mayor. Russell wasn't BSing."

Gamps whispers "Watch your godd*mned mouth Skeet." Halfhearted. Otherwise he would have popped me one upside the head.

"You all right Gamps?"

"I'm all right."

"What's 'By His Bootstraps' mean?"

"Means he wasn't born with no silver spoon in hand. True enough I reckon but I wasn't either and you don't see me boasting about it."

"Oh. What's that mean about a silver spoon?"

"Shut up Skeet."

"All right Gamps. Hey maybe we can hit up that Grease Bros. Pizza buffet for dinner." It's only four o'clock and hot as heck but they keep the Grease Bros. Pizza restaurant well air-conditioned.

He doesn't speak for a while but then says "Fine by me." Something's missing in his voice. Hard to say what. But at last he perks up a bit and says "Yeah I could eat. I could eat. I could eat me some pizza buffet."

We drive back into town and all the while Gamps whispering "Mayor Lingdenberry" under his breath. Same way he whispers "My *ss" about the Real American City sign or "Best Cup Is *Every* Cup" on a morning after drinking. I don't know what's come over him. Gamps likes Mr. Lingdenberry. He's liked him ever since he hired me on as Video Store Clerk at Movie Mayhem back when I was a freshman at Pinehouse High School. He should be happy I suppose happy about the soon-to-be Mayor Lingdenberry. He will be mayor I think. No question about it. Any man who has got himself a cellular phone ought to be mayor 'cause he can get things done anywhere even while driving around in his cherry-red Romulus convertible.

We arrive at the Grease Bros. Pizza on Pinehouse Avenue actually not too far from Movie Mayhem which is convenient in case you want to hit up the buffet for lunch. It's got a big old red roof and they got inside these stained-glass light fixtures and very nice dark-red cups. Iltday cups. And the AC is cranked so high the sweat dries off your back in a matter of seconds soon as you enter and by the time you hit up the buffet you're dry but also a little bit sticky.

We get seated by a nice young lady pale with pigtails sprouting up high atop her head like horns and black lipstick named Shannon. Gamps orders beer with his buffet and I get the soda fountain.

I do all the legwork on account of Stan. Gamps doesn't eat anything but pepperoni but I get sausage too for myself and also the pasta bar which offers fine spaghetti and three different sauces to choose from—Marinara and Meat and Alfredo and I just do a ladle of each right on top of the others. They also got salad with banana peppers and I get some of that too and an Atomic Fizz Neon Lime Flavor (Fear the Fizz). By the time I got all the food to the table Gamps is already starting in on his second Brewster (Another Brewster For You Sir).

"Well. Now. This is quite a feast" I say. What was it Gamps said the other day? "A... repast for kings."

Gamps doesn't hear me. He's quiet for a time. I put down three slices of sausage then I say "Hey Gamps I thought I'd get us a Disney movie." Disney movies are animated musicals categorized in Kids and they're usually pretty funny. "I thought I'd get *Beauty and the Beast*. It's got a talking candlestick and clock in it. Thought that would be pretty good."

"All right" Gamps says. "You get it?"

"No. I thought about it but then forgot to get it. I'll get it Saturday I reckon."

"All right."

"Hey do you think maybe the Scarecrow and the Tin Man and the Cowardly Lion all knew each other before they met Dorothy? I mean they all lived on the same doggone road and I know just about everyone on Sumter Road."

He's staring into his beer.

That pretty much puts the kibosh on the conversation for a few minutes. Kibosh is a word Russell taught me. He's always teaching me sick words in an attempt to make me more hip he says. Sick. Kibosh. Pussy. I'm probably leaving some other words out.

"Miss!" Gamps calls out. He holds up his empty bottle and wags it. Soon another Brewster arrives. Another Brewster For You Sir.

"You ain't eating much Gamps."

"I'm in a drink ponder all right?"

"I'm gonna go get some more Fear the Fizz. You want anything?"

He waves me away. Gamps gets moods I guess is the only way to explain it. He gets moods. Drink ponders. Drink thinks. Drunken I-don't-know-whats. He's got to drive us home though. I'm not allowed behind the wheel of genuine automobiles even if I am twenty-one years old but I can do bumper cars at the State Fair which I did do three years ago the last time we went. And I'm allowed to take the golf cart up and down Sumter Road as long as I promise to avoid the potholes. Plus when Gumma wasn't resting her soul she would take me to the drugstore in downtown Pinehouse where they have this mechanical police car ride in the shade of the awning and you'd put in a quarter and sit in it and it'd shake and rock and you'd get yourself a grape sucker and just have a ball. But aside from that I've never been behind the wheel—except when I busted up Ms. Elsworth's mailbox but I'm not supposed to bring that up—and I don't suppose Gamps ought to drink any more Brewsters For You Sir especially on an empty stomach.

Got to do something about this. Walk up to the hostess with my Atomic Fizz Neon Lime Flavor and plate of second helpings and I look at her for a second.

"Can I help you?"

I was going to say something about Gamps about his drinking and me not being able to drive us home and all that but then I remember that ride that police car ride and the grape suckers Gumma would buy at the drugstore and the way that police car would shake and rock till you about split open and spilled everything out.

"I wet myself once on it" I say.

"Sorry?"

"On that drugstore mechanical police car ride. That black-and-white one. I wet myself on it."

"I'm... I'm sorry?"

I shake my head. "Y'all got grape suckers here?"

"Umm. No?" Sounds like a question when she says it but I reckon it's not.

"All right. I'm gonna go sit down now with Gamps."

She shuffles her feet. I don't recognize the brand of shoes. "Okay?"

Tell you what they got nice folks working at the Grease Bros. Pizza in Pinehouse SC.

What happens next I'm not supposed to tell you about but we go by the King of Hearts and I play *Centipede* for an hour or so a few rolls of quarters and Gamps plops down at the bar and has I don't know how many beers but the drinking goes on and on. When I'm out of quarters I wander outside and kick around stones in the parking lot. Finally around nine or so nearly sundown with the black pine trees shivering beneath a green-tinged sky Gamps staggers out the door and nearly falls over but I catch him and you can smell that beer leaking out of him—I tell you he is crying beer and wiping beer snot—and well even after that we don't get home till pretty late till the stars are all out 'cause we drive all over Pinehouse practically down every road and fill up the back of the Hamtramck with every last doggone Lingdenberry for Mayor – By His Bootstraps sign which is colored red white and blue and has a picture of Mr. Lingdenberry smiling a "smarmy sh*t-eating smile" according to Gamps. The first sign we stop to pick up Gamps gets out staggering and swaying. Then he kicks Stan into it and gets his Reebok shoe jammed in Mr. Lingdenberry's mouth and loses his balance in the process. I get out of the truck and help him up and after that I do all the legwork.

As we turn into Sumter Road I ask Gamps what we're going to do with all those signs in the back. I reckon there's fifty or a hundred of the things sliding and jostling around back there. It's a miracle we weren't spotted taking them all. A miracle the police didn't pull us over and have me spend the night behind bars again.

"Reckon. Reckon. Burn 'em bury 'em something. You lug 'em out back to the 'bandoned lot tomorrow. I had eee-d*mn-nough for today. I'm done beat Jeef Sketcoat. Skeef Jetcoat. Sket you whatever."

"I reckon I'll put a couple in my room."

"Like h*ll you will. That's. Ev'dence. Can't keep ev'dence. Di'pose of it. Prop'ly promptly. We'll take it out. Take it out. That tobacco shed." He laughs. "Burn 'em. Melt 'em. Smelt 'em. I… dunno. Haven't thought. Haven't. Thought that far. Ahead." He belches and looks like he might be sick but the look passes.

"Aw heck Gamps how about just one? Mr. Lingdenberry's my boss and a real swell guy."

He grunts and waves his hand accidentally smacking me in the side of the head. "Won't have that. That b*stard. My house. Not him. Not his accursed semblance. We're home. Get out the d*mned car. Scoot Skeet."

We go in through the carport door and Gamps falls face first onto the kitchen floor. *Thud!* Out cold.

I stand over him for a minute wondering what to do. Maybe eat another dinner. It actually doesn't smell too good in here if I'm perfectly blunt about it. Smells like the dump behind the Burger Braggers. Spoiled meat. Curdled special sauce. I shift Gamps this way and that till I can scoop him up under his armpits and then drag him into his bedroom hoist him up in there and shut the door on my way out.

Back in the kitchen I root around for what all I'm going to eat. Got some old spicy wings from Sunday with Ranch sauce that— yep—still tastes all right and also iced tea and coleslaw and a hard biscuit that fell in the sink but is okay okay okey dokey—time to dinner up a storm.

I reckon I could work some after dinner. Reckon I could write some is what I mean. It's Thursday so it's green pine green a dark but not too dark green sticky green resinous green. If I think real hard it seems to me that it hadn't always been that green was Thursdays. It used to be some other way some colorless way a way you could neither see nor touch. But that other way is all a bit hazy like when the shower had hot water running too long and the mirror gets all fogged up. I can't really see it clear—

Thump.

The sound comes from above me then a bunch of feet running. I can hear them running away over me past me to some distant part of the attic. My heart sinks. Thought we were done with this attic business. I get up from the table and creep around past all the furniture and boxes and piles of things and into the hallway where we got a few cabinets and every edition of the Pinehouse phone book plus a bunch of extra ones we collected from trash bins and seven spare telephones and I pause there and listen.

The scratching starts again. Right over the trapdoor.

—*Please*—

I don't want to go any farther into the hallway so I go on into the living room and I stomp loudly so I can't hear the scratching and I can't hear the voice saying —*Please*— and I stomp my way through to the other end of the living room where another door crosses through the hallway and into my room. I shut the door behind me and slide one of the mattresses in front of it. Then I hear those footsteps again like a bunch of kids three or four I reckon scurrying around running right into the space of the attic above my room and settling down there just a few feet above my head.

I sit down at my desk and click out the green tip of the pen and I pretend like I'm going to study but I don't. I can't. It's like there's a hole in my brain. Through which things flood outward. Out a hole. A different word than whole. 'Cause it isn't whole.

Hole.

Whole.

Hole.

Whole.

The words flip over and over like two sides of a coin in my mind. Like a quarter that slipped from my greasy fingers when I went to put it into the *Centipede* machine.

Chapter 6
Friday

Friday begins with a banging at the door. I run through the house shaking all the cabinets and causing a bit of ceiling popcorn to rain down on everything coated in Friday pink. The doorbell's broken Ma'am in case you were wondering about all the danged knocking. And well looky here if it isn't Mr. Lingdenberry of Movie Mayhem fame.

"By His Bootstraps." That's what I say to him when I open up the screen door.

"Hiya there Skeet. Mind if I come in?" He's one of the tallest men in the town. Taller than his son Russell but not taller than me. I reckon that's why he hired me on as Video Store Clerk at Movie Mayhem on account of my height and my alphabetizing skill plus my knowledge of Musicals (you better believe every last danged musical is ordered properly in the Musicals section). He has his hair swooped back. Blondish white unlike his son Russell and his greasy dark lanky hair. And he wears suits baby-blue suits and ties of different-colored stripes everywhere he goes. Heck I bet he mows the lawn in a suit. I bet he showers in a suit. On top of all that he never swears. An honest-to-God gentleman.

"Suit yourself." I was thinking about suits. Maybe that's why I say it like that like "suit yourself" instead of some other old way.

He steps inside and his feet crinkle all the plastic wrappers from that time that I ate an entire box of Duchess Ruby Jam Cakes by the screen door watching something out in the yard. I think it was the lawn ornaments I was watching or maybe seeing what all the neighbors were putting out on trash day or what Deidre Thomas was up to I couldn't tell you what the heck it was I was doing but the Ruby Jam Cake wrappers remain.

"My y'all have a fine place here." His eyes are looking every which way. There's a lot to see.

"Yessir. I may as well show you the televisions 'cause we have nine of the danged things. Ten actually. I forgot the Azimuth we found yesterday. Think it was yesterday." I count my colors on my fingers. "Nah that was two days ago."

"Aha. Y'all have quite a collection of... quite a collection."

"None of them work but the Lumovox."

He follows me over to the stacks of televisions and I see the two of us reflected in the dark gray of the screens each of the images curved like we were drawn on the surfaces of a bunch of eyeballs.

"You like it there at Movie Mayhem Skeet Jeffcoat Deveaux?"

I nod. "Yessir." What I like is how he says Movie Mayhem and Skeet Jeffcoat Deveaux side by side like that. Like we are one and inseparable. Twins me and a building a place of business.

He places a hand on my shoulder.

"Does Russell treat you all right?"

I nod. "Yessir." We fight a good bit but it's a bit complicated I suppose 'cause after all we're pretty good buddies even if he does have the worst potty mouth there ever was.

"I know about the tussle y'all had but I sorted Russell out—sorted everything out. He's an emotional young man. Can't control himself sometimes. Given to expressing his anger in wholly inappropriate ways. Never you mind about him. Now. I was thinking it's about time I gave you a raise a... uh promotion. What do you say to that?"

"I reckon that's okay. If you got the capital."

He laughs and gives my arm a squeeze. "Oh heck now you know I do boy. I'm making you my Video Rental Associate. How does that sound?"

"Finer than than than than the Emerald City I reckon."

"'Finer than the Emerald City.' I like that. You mind if I use that line?"

"Heck I don't care." I'm staring at his shiny brown shoes. Must be the finest shoes in Pinehouse.

"All right then. Now. Listen. You want to go get Jasper there… go get your Gamps for me? The two of us need to have a little heart-to-heart." His hand moves off my arm and goes to his chest which he gives a little squeeze like he's massaging a heart growing there. His fingers are long and have shining silver rings.

"Yessir." I make my way over to the hallway when Mr. Lingdenberry calls out to me.

"Skeet?"

"Yessir?"

"You're a well-mannered boy. I'm. Proud to have you. On the Movie Mayhem team."

I smile big and turn down the hallway and go down to Gamps's room and bang on the flimsy door. It's about paper thin. I could bash it in with a baseball bat and storm in there if there was ever a need. "Gamps! Gamps! Get up!"

"What the High H*ll?" He's got the groggy sound of a morning after a big drinking night.

"Mr. Lingdenberry's here."

He makes some more noises which I can't repeat because number one I don't understand half of it and number two it would be criminal for me to repeat what I do manage to understand. The door swings inward and Gamps pushes past me and he's not wearing any pants if you get my meaning which is that he is wearing boxer shorts and his favorite t-shirt with the flames and you can see his stump fitting into Stan which is not something you see too often in this household no Ma'am. I can smell the old beer and cigarettes on him and it is not a pretty smell.

"What'd I tell you last night you nitwit?" He pops me across the face. "I won't have that 'By His Bootstraps' jackanapes in my house. That's what I said. Even drunk my memory's better than yours you d*mn fool." He shoves past me and limps through the hall around the bend and into the living room.

"What's that supposed to mean about His Bootstraps?" I say following behind.

Gamps wheels back around towards me. For a moment I think he's going to hit me I mean really clobber me. But he stops himself. "Get your godd*mned sorry *ss into your room and try to learn some f*cking sense!"

I stand there shoulders slumping and hear Gamps storm in on Mr. Lingdenberry. "Bit hard on the boy aren't you?" This is what Mr. Lingdenberry says instead of "Hello Gamps good morning nice to see you."

"What the h*ll you doing in my house?"

"You tell me Jasper."

I shouldn't stand here and listen I know that but I can't bring myself to move can't lift one danged combat boot. The air is thick. Gravity heavy. Hot as Hades (that's a nicer way to say heck or h*ll). Oughtta go to my room. Oughtta.

"Don't know what the h*ll you're talking about."

"Got the boy up to doing all kinds of dirty work for you. Theft of political campaign signs. That's a misdemeanor offense in the State of South Carolina."

"Get the f*ck outta my house!"

"Oughtn't you to show a bit more respect towards Skeet's meal ticket?"

"Meal ticket!? Bah!"

"I'm gonna make it easy on you Jasper. Y'all put the signs back and I make sure no one presses charges. A'ight?"

"I'll give you to the count of three to show me your backside before I get my 12-gauge."

Mr. Lingdenberry chuckles. "Listen up. Got witnesses Jasper. Several of them. Called me up all last night. Had the cops calling too. I don't think you realize the seriousness of what y'all were doing. People a bit lenient on y'all. Given y'all's circumstances."

I shouldn't be listening to this I think. It doesn't sound like the kind of thing Gamps wants me hearing.

"They saw the big boy—heck everyone in town knows Skeet Jeffcoat Deveaux—and your truck. Forest-green Hamtramck rusted with love."

I move towards my room and Gamps and Mr. Lingdenberry stop talking. The floors are making a racket and the furniture is rattling a bit with every step the inlaid glass windows of the cabinet doors and all those ceramic elves that Gumma collected. She didn't like a busy house but she did collect those little ceramic figures. They shake and clink with every step staring at me with their big eyes and smiling mouths saying in high-pitched chorus "We see you Skeet we see you were eavesdropping." Even when I walk slow and careful the way Gamps is always telling me to and holding my breath the whole house knows and reports every danged twitch of my muscles.

In my room I can still hear them talking but not as loud as before. I put on my headphones and turn on an audio recording of *The Wizard of Oz* from last week and soon I hear Dorothy scuttling around the farmhouse talking to Toto and me in the foreground describing to Gamps what all I like about the beginning of the movie and how Sunday gray isn't all that bad how it can be kind of comforting sometimes. You never hear anyone in the movie mention what day of the week it is but I guess it's pretty obvious.

Anyway I can no longer make out Gamps and Mr. Lingdenberry's conversation.

As it should be.

Everyone In Town Knows Skeet Jeffcoat Deveaux.

Everyone In Town Knows Skeet Jeffcoat Deveaux.

I smile thinking about what Mr. Lingdenberry said and look out the window at the summer day which fades to pink every which way you look. It's what you get if you let the ice melt in your pink lemonade and it's all watery and translucent at the surface but getting pinker and pinker as you sink down. That's the Friday I know the Friday every week.

So I click out the pink tip of my 10-Color Pen.

Everyone In Town Knows Skeet Jeffcoat Deveaux.

Everyone In Town Knows Skeet Jeffcoat Deveaux

Skeet Jeffcoat Deveaux

Skeet Jeffcoat Deveaux

Skeet Jeffcoat Deveaux

Everyone In Town Knows

Deidre Thomas is not out back today and all the blinds of her windows are always closed so you can never really see anything in them but the edges of light at night sometimes. Still I got work to do today and so after writing my name for a few pages I think up a real good story about how it's Friday and Mayor Lingdenberry in honor of my promotion takes it upon himself to come over to my house with all the other Movie Mayhem employees even the ones I don't normally see the ones that work evenings Thursdays and Saturdays and all the other days of the week employees I couldn't even begin to tell you about because I've never been to Movie Mayhem on those other days. In this story all the employees look a bit like Russell Lingdenberry except their shirts are different colors for the different days and they come on over and knock at the door and I say "Hold on a second I'm just getting up!" and tear away the top page of the daily calendar and today's meditation is…

Well what is today's meditation? Actually I forgot to do that today and to tell you the truth I can't remember the last time I tore off a day so I get up from my desk and root around for it and find it stuffed between my mattress and the wall and tear off Wednesday and Thursday but because the paper's all stuck together it tears up Friday and the next day leaving all the letters messed up. Can't hardly read it but it looks like Iltday. No meditation either or date. All that information ripped from the surface of the paper leaving behind the pulpy texture underneath like the paper was skinned.

Well.

That.

Stinks.

I don't know how in the heck to work that into the story so I write that word Iltday over and over to try and see what comes.

Iltday Iltday Iltday Iltday

The audio recording ends and it seems Gamps is in his bedroom 'cause I hear the familiar soothing rhythm of the Happy Value Shopping channel.

Guess it's all right to come out now.

Yup.

It's business as usual at the Deveaux Household. Breakfast and Calders. The whole nine yards. Gamps has already nodded off by the time I come in but the smell of the bacon and coffee rouses him.

No talking at first. Just the Happy Value Shopping product line. A few interesting things some of them repeated from earlier this week like the Deluxe Cat Tree then these modern-looking lamps show up which you just touch and they turn on.

"Like magic" the blonde woman in the pink dress says every time she touches one.

"Now look here Skeet Jeffcoat this is what I call a solid investment" Gamps says perking up for the first time this morning.

Brass twenty-inch tip-touch they keep calling the lamps. Like magic. Gamps takes down notes on the product as he eats his waffles and bacon.

"Hey Gamps you sore at Mr. Lingdenberry?"

"What the h*ll you think?"

"I think yes."

"Well hot dog Skeet Jeffcoat Deveaux there's hope for you yet."

I laugh at this and Gamps eventually laughs too but only after staring at me slantwise a moment.

"We going to go out and bury those election signs? We could stash them in the old abandoned tobacco shed like you said."

Gamps grunts.

"Does that mean yes?"

"Means I haven't rightly decided Skeet."

Well breakfast was a clear success I think as I'm clearing all the dishes out of the bedroom. I go back and forth from Gamps's bedroom and the kitchen and because I'm feeling good because Everyone In Town Knows Skeet Jeffcoat Deveaux I ask Gamps if he will be wanting his Another Brewster For You Sir given that it's Friday.

"No no I don't reckon so. I'm done drinking. From this day forward. Mark my words. Just top off my Calders for me. Best D*mn Cup Is *Every* Cup."

I whisper this last part under my breath as Gamps says it except I don't use the word d*mn and so his voice doesn't quite match up with my lips just like they didn't in that Lucio Fulci movie Russell had on the other day.

"Quit parroting me and get the doggone coffee Skeet Jeffcoat."

I take his coffee mug back to the kitchen and let me tell you about this mug because it says Myrtle Beach on it in dark blue cursive but the letters are all erased from where Gamps has repeatedly put his lips to it and also has several beautiful women in bikinis lined up and each bikini is a different color blue and green and yellow and orange and pink and it makes my head spin because it's very nearly the colors of the week but moving in the wrong doggone direction a bit of a mindf*ck as Russell Lingdenberry would say.

There are things moving all around the kitchen and the smell is worse than ever before. It's a rotten sickly-sweet smell that might make me gag if I weren't so used to it. In addition to the palmetto bugs I find a line of fire ants coming in from somewhere and heading for the cabinet under the sink where I sometimes stash leftovers when the indoor fridge is full up which is more frequently than you might think. Fire ants are trouble but you just got to let them do their thing that's how Gumma taught me. There are things growing under there. Mold and fungus big domes of it the white and yellow of fried eggs and blue-gray stalactites drooping down. And I hear scurrying too but it's above me like it was before. In the attic. Then the scratching starts up really vigorous and fast.

Squirrels Gamps said. We had decided days ago it was squirrels but there are other possibilities. Really big palmetto bugs. Giant ones. Rat-sized palmetto bugs. Maybe bigger.

I pour the Calders but my arm is shaking and the coffee spills a little and scalds my hand. I cuss. I do. I admit it. Then sop it up sop up the mess and bring the mug back down the hall when—

—*Please please please please*—

Gamps is suddenly gripping my shoulders and it looks like I dropped the danged Myrtle Beach mug and spilled the Calders all over the carpet but fortunately the mug and bikini beauties survived the fall though there's quite the mess a big brown stain still warm.

"You okay Skeet?" Gamps is saying unsteady on Stan. He finally got his jeans on and his favorite t-shirt and I got on my favorite t-shirt and my jean shorts on and my boots are sticking in the coffee puddle. We're quite the pair.

"Why you shaking me Gamps?"

"You were talking some nonsense. Eyes rolled back into your head. Reciting the days of the week... but... not all proper days. It was some kind of fit I reckon. Ain't had one of them since... well it's been a while."

"I'll clean up the mess Gamps. Wasted your Calders. Dang it!" I feel a little angry about the Calders.

"Don't worry about that. I'll get the coffee." Gamps gets his mechanical grabber from the bedroom and picks up the mug with it and walks to the kitchen. Pretty nifty that grabber.

I'm staring at the coffee stain shaking my head.

"You remember what you were saying?" Gamps calls from the kitchen. "Talking about Iltday."

I can't hear the scratching anymore. I look up at the pull down. The ceiling's so low and I'm so tall I could pull on the cord right now. The attic door would open the ladder would unfold. But I'm not supposed to.

"Skeet I'm talking to you boy."

"Yeah Gamps." I walk over to the kitchen.

"Why you talking about Iltday again?"

"'Cause it's one of the days of the week. It's the red day."

Gamps scoffs at that. "You and your accursed color schemes. Look at the calendar on the wall over there. Go on. Do it."

It's the calendar for 1995 the year I graduated high school at nineteen on account I spent that extra year learning as much as I could from Mrs. Kelly.'95 Staying Alive. It was also the year all those people died including Gumma and the calendar wasn't ever turned over to August from July 'cause it was usually Gumma who did that. She always kept a calendar here. This one's the Southern Beach Sunset Calendar 1995 and July features Edisto Beach with a black-and-red sunset and a giant oak tree with its roots lifting out of the red sand and black water like some kind of enormous knobby squid except it has tentacles coming out of the top of its head too where the branches are leafless of course 'cause the thing's dead long long dead.

"Read them off to me. Read me the days of the week" Gamps says. Orders is more like it. He's calm now but might be any moment he'll explode at me.

I step close. God it stinks in here. God Almighty.

I can read of course. I can write. I can read. I can do arithmetic. There are some things wrong with me Gamps says (and I believe him) but it isn't an inability to write and read and do arithmetic. I can read the titles of the movies at Movie Mayhem 'cause I can shelve the movies and I can read the section signs hanging down on chains from the ceiling 'cause I can direct customers to the Drama and the Musicals. 'Cause. I can. I can make change for rentals. Three dollars for a New Release and one dollar for everything else and if you give me five dollars and want to rent one New Release—

"Read it Skeet!"

"Sunday Monday Tuesday Wednesday Thursday Friday."

I pause for some reason here and stare at the side-by-side boxes. Something's wrong. Something's wrong. It starts with Sunday which is right no matter what it should always start with Sunday but then towards the end—

"Go on."

"Friday Friiiiiday." I'm a bit stuck between boxes but then at last manage to move on. "Saturday." That's the end of the row so I stop again and for good this time but there's also something wrong at the end of the row because... because... why now?

"You see any piffle called Iltday there?"

I shake my head. "No Gamps. Nosir."

"Good. As it should be. Maybe you don't remember it in that foggy head of yours but I do I remember. Every time hurricane season comes around you get to talking about Iltday or some such. Well I don't want to hear no more about it. Gave me the creeps back there. Gives me the creeps every time I hear that word."

Except there is an Iltday
doesn't always come but when
it does it comes twice twice
in a week and when it
comes there's no moon and when it
comes there's no sun
no stars in the
deep red sky in
the deep
deep

Beyond our property line in the backyard is the old field growing nothing now but briars and itchy grass and while we got a chain-link fence dividing the land a pine tree grew against it and swelled up and knocked the top bar loose and now all the chain is sagging and even I can squeeze through and as Everyone In Town Knows I'm a big boy big even for a twenty-one-year-old grown adult.

Back there a dirt road leads to the tobacco shed but it's all over-grown now so overgrown you could barely tell it was there even if you knew where it was. There're all kinds of scrub pine and poison ivy growing in the woods there up on a hill surrounded by a field which Gamps says once upon a time was used for growing tobacco and later on the farm turned to cotton but now the landowner is dead and it's all overgrown too and yes the owner died around the same time Gumma died in case you were wondering. The police called it a killing spree and there were a number of articles in the *Pinehouse Chronicle* and believe it or not I got to go to the police station and see the inside of a jail cell then I spent a lot of time in a room with three officers wearing polo shirts and khakis (they were called Rhett and Marnie and then the guy who didn't speak was Chip) who kept handing me bottles of Atomic Fizz Neon Lime Flavor (Fear the Fizz) and chocolate-frosted custard-filled donuts from Dunno Donuts while letting me talk about just about whatever I wanted to talk about and they even asked me about of all things the shotgun Gamps keeps in the upper cabinet of his bureau his pine-wood bureau that he doesn't like me to touch and where had Gamps gone that weekend and didn't it seem like a strange coincidence that he chose to go hunting that particular weekend especially since it wasn't even hunting season and could Gamps even reasonably go out hunting with his leg like it was? Tell you what. I was real danged confused by all the questions. But I tell you what I ate about a thousand chocolate-frosted custard-filled donuts during my stay at the Pinehouse Police Station.

It's a hot day and the cicadas are whining and sawing so loud you can't even hear the traffic from the Sandhills Highway. We took a lot of those election signs and I can't carry but a few on each trip. Well it would have been better if Gamps could drive me up to the tobacco shed but as I mentioned to you the road's all overgrown and besides I don't want to bother Gamps 'cause it's plain as day that the signs rattle him. I thought I would just decide for him. Take them on up there just as he suggested last night after Grease Bros. Pizza and all that drinking.

I stare into the truck bed for a long time looking at all those By His Bootstraps signs and decide I will bring them all to the fence first and then we'll see what's what. It takes me ten trips I count them and I'm all sweaty and huffing by the end of it. Lord you can't hardly breathe in this heat and humidity. It's a bit complicated to move around back here because of all the aisle shelves we took from the Rhoda's Discount Store that closed down plus all kinds of other appliances and tools that we couldn't fit in the carport.

For example we got twenty-odd plastic storage bins and some spare lamps and a washer/dryer and various pieces of furniture including two couches which smell ripe with mildew and table legs as well as full proper tables plus a whole bunch of wood 2x4s for building with 'cause Gamps is planning out this whole new addition to our house which will go back all the way to the chainlink and which will be half storage space and half games room 'cause Gamps says back in Korea he was the Snooker King and if you are wondering if we have a snooker table yes Ma'am we do three of them but the felt is all ripped on one and the surface is all warped on another and one table has only got one and a half legs "Just like me" Gamps had said as I loaded it into the back of the Hamtramck last year during one of our Treasure Cruises. He said he reckons he's handy with tools and can take all the good parts from each table and put them together into a real beauuuute but right now they're on their sides with tarps over them.

Yes Ma'am we got our work cut out for us.

Eventually I get all the signs down beyond the chain link and carry them across the field where scratchy pine saplings have taken root and reach up to my belly. You got to move fast out here on account of the fire ants and the cow ants which are like wasps with their wings plucked off them and with Iltday-red stripes and a little bit fuzzy and can sting you powerful enough to kill a human or a horse or a cow. Hence the name.

The ground slopes up to the woods. Then there's the shed itself hidden in the trees almost a part of the woods itself like it was grown here and not built by man. It's a convenient place 'cause no one much comes out this way. The roof is caved in partways. No door or windows. There's no tobacco but there's pine. Got a brush of saplings and one tree that made it all the way up past the rafters and through the roof. Got poison ivy every which way climbing up the walls and through the crevices in the walls. Kudzu too. That's another thing we got a lot of in Pinehouse.

Also plenty of spiders which give me the heebie-jeebies. Wolf spiders mostly. Fast and hairy. I don't stand inside too long 'cause if you do a wolf spider might hop onto you or worse. I've never been bit by a wolf spider and don't want to thank you very much.

Well in total it takes a few hours of lugging and dragging and carrying and cussing once (sorry Ma'am I didn't mean to) 'cause one of the plastic signs cut my left palm open and I smeared blood all over Mr. Lingdenberry's name. But I take breaks and do all kinds of other things in between getting sidetracked with eating and making an "Achy Breaky Heart" mixtape and everything so it's actually pretty late in the day when all is said and done. I didn't get bitten by a spider though which I'm grateful for and when I'm standing out there at the edge of the woods getting ready to go back down for the last time today I can see farther than usual 'cause all of Pinehouse is perfectly flat except for a few hills around where we live. You can just see downtown from here—EAT and the Slash Spree and Main Street and the really tiny Burger Braggers sign of a burger eating a man's head—and farther over is the biggest crucifix in SC bathed in the pink of today and the skyline over everything is cotton candy the big billowing pink kind and for a moment a red tinge swirls through it the way blood does in water and vanishes just as quick leaving behind the same vibrant pink as before and I linger there a few minutes waiting to see if it will show again.

The cicadas are ratcheting up something ferocious and I am dripping with sweat and my favorite t-shirt has turned see-through.

I may have imagined it. That red. Gamps says I imagine things sometimes. Specifically what he says is I'm about 99 parts imagination and 1 part sense.

Sure enough the sky doesn't redden again.

Back home I find Gamps is gone.

That's all right.

Got to do some danged cleaning in this pigsty as Gamps would say. Reckon that my room is as good a place as any to start. I shift around the mattresses first because if I'm honest about it they take up more room than anything else in here but then I think maybe it might be nice to unwind with some Bounce House and so I start ramming into them and rebounding off one and into the next. My head starts spinning and an air of lightness and joy rises up from inside me and I just can't help it but I need to sing something and that something turns out to be "Ding-Dong! The Witch Is Dead." I just belt it out as loud as I can. "Ding Dong! Ding Dong! Ding Dong! Ding Dong!"

The front door slams shut and I can hear from the lopsided footsteps that Gamps is home so I quit bouncing around and run out there hitting the walls and almost falling over from the dizziness. "Hi Gamps!"

He startles. "Christ Almighty who let the rhino out of its cage?"

Getting up I laugh big time. "It's just me Gamps."

"I see that. Got us our repast." He raises a white paper bag from Hudson's Subs and Grub. I smell fries and oil and vinegar. Hot dang.

"Get out the TV trays. Don't feel like eating in that disgrace of a kitchen. Let's set up in the living room."

"Yessir Gamps."

He settles into the recliner and I get everything all set up. We got Italian subs soggy with oil and glistening fries salted generously.

"Grab me that remote there Skeet Jeffcoat. Time for the evening news. See if they mention Danny."

We eat and watch. The onions are so powerful and piled so thick they make you cry.

"Downgraded to a tropical storm but it's coming for us all right" Gamps says. "You hear that? Tomorrow evening they say. Got to make preparations. Going to be a circus at the grocery store."

"I reckon so."

"These fries are making me thirsty. How about going out to get Gamps a Brewster."

"A'ight" I say it like Mr. Lingdenberry said it earlier today hoping Gamps would laugh but he doesn't. "Another Brewster For You Sir."

"Go on now Mr. Skeet."

"Welp. All right." But I don't really want to. Don't know if I mentioned it to you before but I don't like going into the backyard at night. It's 'cause we got so much stuff and it's a maze of stuff I suppose and the shadows are thick. One time I came across a possum when I went to go fetch a beer for Gamps and when it hissed at me like a snake its eyes glowing in the dark I dropped my flashlight and hightailed it back inside and got a dressing-down from Gamps about how ridiculous it is for a big lunk like myself to be scared of a little night critter. "You want to listen to some Kenny Rogers or 'Electric Boogie' or something like that?"

"Just the beer Skeet Jeffcoat."

"You want me to make us some Waffacombs or something like that?"

He cocks his head and gives me a hard look. "You hear what I said?"

"All right Gamps." I go through the kitchen flies buzzing around and palmetto bugs scattering. In the laundry room I root around one of the cabinets and my hand settles on an old hammer with a broken claw and for a moment I think I remember how it was broken remember seeing it swing down and strike something but the moment passes and I see the flashlight in back and grab that instead.

The heat is something horrendous outside. The air is so thick and hot it's like breathing soup. Though it's dark by now the western horizon is alive with heat lightning not the quick purple of normal summertime but with slow red fissures crackling down from wherever Iltday comes from. I feel a little edgy inside a little nervous about it and I barrel through the stacks of refrigerators and grab a six-pack then hightail it back inside and slam the door shut behind me. The red glow outside is growing but it's not here yet. Dang it it's coming though.

Gamps guzzles his beer and I shovel all the food in my mouth that'll fit. Boy howdy. Boy howdy. Can see the color growing now behind the closed blinds that deep red eclipsing the pink.

It'll be soon now. Soon. Soon. Soon.

I sit rocking on the couch while Gamps downs his beers and scratches Stan now and again. I should've gotten more than a six-pack. He'll be through it in no time. The television plays on all the while unaware that Iltday is almost upon us.

"Hold your horses Skeet Jeffcoat. We made it! Must've been a slow news day."

The local news has come on and there's Ms. Paige O'Connor of WNMB-TV interviewing my boss and future mayor of Pinehouse Mr. Lingdenberry who is saying that he is not disheartened by the thefts of the political signs and is working to have the issue resolved privately without involving the authorities. His eyes are all pink and featureless and thick streams of bubble-gum-colored tears are flowing down his face and staining his jacket.

"Oh gee Gamps. Look at how upset he is about the signs. I didn't want to make Mr. Lingdenberry cry."

"What the h*ll you talking about? I don't see any tears. Same old snake in a suit."

"Why don't you like that Mr. Lingdenberry? He's a good boss. Russell Lingdenberry ain't half bad half the time neither."

"Not half bad half the time makes him what a quarter good?"

This gets an uneasy laugh from me though I don't know what the heck he's talking about. Truth is I'm having trouble looking away from the window and that slow dawn of red.

"He's a liar Skeet Jeffcoat. A slimy no-good prevaricator. You tell him I said so too." He shakes his head. "You never got the chance to really know your Mama. Your sweet Mama. D*mn shame Skeet Jeffcoat. Never really knew her. Bless her dear heart. Prettiest girl in Pinehouse."

Not sure why he jumps from Mr. Lingdenberry to talking about my mother but it's true what Gamps says about her. She gave birth to me and yet I didn't really know her all that much. A memory or two. Maybe from pictures I saw of her or things that actually happened to me. We do have a family photo album and in it there's a picture of yours truly Skeet Jeffcoat Deveaux at a birthday party and there's my mother in a white dress and long black ponytail setting the cake on the table. Her skin is a little dark like Gamps's and she's got big dimples and the candle on the cake is the number 6 and in my memory the edges are framed in white and frayed and the colors are faded and there are a series of sunspots cast over us like the multiple suns in *Star Wars*. And for some reason you can't tell what day it was no color to go by.

"This calls for a celebration Skeet Jeffcoat. One more Brewster sir."

He's finally through the six-pack.

I don't want to go out there but I guess there's no way around it.

I go out back and it's night no longer.

It's a new day.

Chapter 7
Iltday

I have mentioned to you about the colors of the days of the week and well you can even see those colors when it's nighttime or when you really think hard about what day of the week it is. But Iltday is different. Stronger somehow the red seeps into everything it pricks the surface of things and fills them up and then pools out like blood and it lifts off into the air in a curling mist and the sky is like cooling lava just the red bubbling and blackening and dripping down onto the world.

This is what I see when I step outside to get Gamps's Brewster. I check my Chronometrix Radio-Glo Watch and see that the time is blinking between 77:77:77 and 99:99:99 which makes sense because Iltday is both the seventh and ninth day of the week. 'Cause it comes twice.

Deidre Thomas's ginger cat is out here frozen in place and jittering. An X-ray of a cat with its bones glowing a hot red-orange and its skin translucent and strings of smoke radiating off its body pearl white dashed with blood. For some reason my skin isn't translucent the way Deidre Thomas's cat's is and I remember it's always this way when Iltday comes. I'm the only one moving around.

The backyard seems larger now with all of our Treasure Cruise finds spaced out a bit more comfortably than it had been before. The way everything looks now spacious and orderly reminds me of the neat rows of tombstones in the First Baptist Church of Pinehouse cemetery. Looks like we had planned it this way like we knew how it would rearrange and order would spring into existence.

Beyond our yard towards that abandoned farm the world ends and a massive void stretches out but floating in it black against all the red is the little wooded hill where the tobacco shed is and floating in another island is the old farmhouse and beyond that Sandhills Highway is a bridge thin and precarious arcing over the emptiness with dirt crumbling from its underside.

I can walk comfortably between the refrigerators and it doesn't smell the same back here as it did before. The stench is much worse much more putrid than it had been. This is what I've been smelling all week I reckon. I smelled Iltday coming the way Gamps can feel a storm coming from the aching and itching sensation inside Stan. All week long I've been smelling this day approaching—

Scratch.

—and hearing it too.

I grab the beers. The smoke from inside the fridge is purple and red and the letters on the cans are all scrambled into "Brweestr" as if the words had been spun around and all the consonants flung out to their edges.

Scratch scratch scratch.

The sound is louder and more frantic than it had been before. It feels close the way it sounds if you scratch your neck right under your ear the sound crawling along your skin and up each and every hair. I don't feel any nails on my neck but I swat at it anyway just to check before running back inside although I don't think it'll help any I don't think it'll be different any I don't think it'll be anything else inside but Iltday.

The laundry room is dark and long longer than it had been before and the shadows deeper the shadows so deep that I could probably walk into them and just walk forever in shadow. My flickering flashlight beam barely cuts through that dark thickness thick darkness so I just focus on the doorway ahead and walk forward breathing hard and unsteady.

Into the kitchen.

It's a different room. Yet also similar to the one in our house. Everything is here but it's spaced out so much. The linoleum doesn't stretch to fill in the space. Just sits there under our table and ends a long way off from the cabinets and walls revealing a fine marble floor beneath it which fills in all the extra space. Again the change of space adds a sense of organization that we lacked but now that I see it I wonder if perhaps I had known all along and had filled this place with so much stuff because I knew there was something lying beneath it an area unseen. My lack of surprise. That's how I know I knew. Strange that I don't remember it so clearly how this all happened on the last Iltday but I'm not surprised by it one bit.

But I do remember something else. About Iltday. And this something gives me pause.

Scratch scratch scratch.

Last time it was Iltday people died around here. Mysterious deaths. They all thought it was me or maybe Gamps and gave us both a ride downtown to the police station for a night or two while they searched our house. They said I knew things about the murder scenes that no one could have guessed like how Ms. Elsworth was attacked in her kitchen when she was feeding her cat the same fat ginger one that Deidre Thomas now feeds. Must be why they wanted to talk to me. Because I knew more than anyone else.

Gumma. Mr. and Mrs. Thomas. Ms. Elsworth. That old man Mr. Lyles in the now-abandoned farmhouse who was always shouting at me to quit walking through his property. Also his wife. I knew where each one had died: Gumma in the carport and the Thomases in their bedroom and Ms. Elsworth in her kitchen and Mr. Lyles in the front room of his house. Mrs. Lyles in their car while she was parking in the driveway.

That was all. Of. Them dead. All six. I think.

Story goes that whoever did it used Hurricane Allison for cover when no one could phone for help but it wasn't done by firearm or shop tool or anything else the police could find so they never did catch the killer. So Gamps and I got to return home.

I walk across the kitchen across that marble floor like something you'd see in *Lifestyles of the Rich and Famous*. Moving quiet and careful and stop at the doorway hesitating before looking into the hallway where there'd normally be all kinds of bureaus and bookshelves and lamps and things and of course the pull down.

Well it's all there but it's not some hallway jam-packed and homey. It's a vast open area like the foyer of some mansion. Makes you think we didn't cram nearly enough things in here. And everything has that Iltday color bleeding out of it and roiling on the floor in a hungry mist. The ceiling is much too high for our house and where the pull down would normally be is a flight of marble stairs.

Scratch scratch scratch.

The sounds are running over me like ants but I can tell it's not as simple as being inside me or being inside the pull down. It's both somehow. I can't explain how I know but I understand that in a few minutes' time I will be climbing those steps like in that television program I watched or the dream or whatever it was and then I'll be at the top and the sound will be closer and not so irksome and then my hand will be on the iron latch and then I'll be lifting it and then—

Shaking the image out of my mind I cross the hall.

Normally two steps to cross it but now it takes twenty or so. In the living room is… well it's not our living room. Doesn't even seem like living room is the right word for it. Probably there's another word. Salon. Parlor. Something fancy like that.

But Gamps is there. Frozen just like my neighbor and best friend Deidre Thomas's cat. Translucent with the bones glowing like they're heating elements inside the toaster oven. And where Stan is you can see how he's missing bones how he's an incomplete person. Same as with his bad hand with the finger nubs.

I place the Brweestr at his feet.

"Gamps" I whisper.

He doesn't move or answer. Except for the jittering if you want to call that movement which I do not thank you very much. It's not like moving it's like the little flipbook cartoons we made in All-Star Class one time where you draw a stick man and move him bit by bit with each drawing and then when you flip through the book he looks like he is running or digging or dancing or pooping or talking except that Gamps looks like the one I drew which did not move at all because I just drew the same stick man in the same position who looked a bit like the "If I Only Had A Brain" Scarecrow but he didn't move because I didn't make him move but he jittered a bit I guess because my drawings weren't exactly in the same spots on the pages.

I touch Gamps again. Say his name. But he's stuck there the bag of bones.

Scratch scratch scratch.

The bugs are crawling over my head and I hunch my shoulders to try and make the sound stop the tingling and itching the horrible sensations that I know would stop once and for all if I just bounded up there and did the deed.

"I gotta do it Gamps" I say scratching at my ears and scalp. "I gotta open that pull down." I still call it a pull down even though it isn't even though all along it hasn't been a pull down but a door a big old iron door with a texture like the inside of a beehive all honeycombed. "I'm gonna climb those stairs Gamps and open it." As I say the words I think how familiar they sound to me like it was the chorus of "Somewhere Over the Rainbow" from the greatest movie of all time or from Billy Ray Cyrus's "Achy Breaky Heart."

Red washes over everything and I realize that I'm already standing at the door and the house is stretching away below me. A chill radiates from the door. A biting chill the kind you only get a couple days out of the year in SC.

My hand touches the latch and it's cold too with a strange shape not meant for my hand. Don't know what the heck kind of hand it's designed for but I turn it and the door groans open.

Everything beyond is dark too dark for eyes to see. Yet if I look into it long enough and hard enough I can see forms churning. Cogs and shifting parts. Gigantic and grinding wheels creating a low rumble. Wheels made of bone—of skulls and fingers and ribs and legs and animal parts too all kinds. Kinds you could imagine or kinds you've seen on TV but also kinds you couldn't kinds you didn't know could exist animals maybe that you would only see in a dream or nightmare.

I want to shut my eyes but am afraid to. Everything beyond the door is in motion. Twisting. Tightening. Winding up. Sliding forward. Retreating. I can't quite make it out make out what's what or where I would end up if I stepped across the threshold. Is that elongated skull with the horns branching and curling out of it floating right before my eyes or is it miles away? The bones seem to caress my skin but they are so tiny and dark and far away that it's impossible they could be this close to scrape up against me.

The door has swung inward into this hall of bones so I can't shut it without reaching inside which doesn't seem like a good idea. It seems like I would get caught by a wheel or spring or something and my arm would be bone-crushed inside there. It seems like the kind of thing Gamps would shout at me about. "Skeet don't you have any d*mn sense? What were you thinking walking into the Hall of Bones?"

I believe if I just reach across the threshold the mechanism of bones would seize me and yank me all the way inside and rip me apart and fix my bones into the gaps of the wheels.

—*Thank you.*—

Something brushes past me. Takes me a moment before I realize what has happened and when I turn I catch a glimpse of something at the base of the stairs but it's so far down now for the height of the stairs must have grown while I was standing up here. So far down it's just a pinprick in my vision.

A pale pinprick.

A pale I-don't-know-what.

The door slams shut behind me and at the same time I feel another door swinging open in my mind and suddenly my legs give out. I start to fall forward and sleep catches me like a swinging hammock and guides me away from the sharp angles of the marble steps.

Chapter 8
Saturday

It's Saturday and have I mentioned the swimming purple things like pale fishes on Saturdays to you? Each color of the week you see has a bit more to it than what you might think. I mentioned how the blue on Wednesday does something I can't now remember can't remember or describe it when I'm not actually experiencing it which is why I'm always writing in my notebooks if I'm perfectly honest with you. Will have to wait till it comes around again before I can be sure. Wednesday's color sprays or flows maybe. I don't know. My head is not working right this morning. The purple fish-things are every-God-darned-where except where I'm looking 'cause when I try to look at one it poofs out of existence but when I look away it comes back together in a drippy dewy way by which I mean a bunch of purple drops gather together in an instant pooling until it's the same size as before and it goes on swimming around. They're always in the corner of my eye and you can't wise up and trap them in a jar or with a net or anything like that but believe you me I have tried plenty of times.

When I'm alone.

Gamps saw me going after them once and when I told him I was trying to catch the Saturday Fish he about had a fit wondering if *I* was having some kind of a fit. It was pretty danged funny and I had quite a laugh and he eventually smiled and laughed too shaking his head the way he does. That's the thing about Gamps. He'll be all serious saying "Skeet you got to this" and "Skeet you got to that" but then when I grin and laugh he can't control himself sometimes and will likely as not join in. 'Cause if you think about anything long enough it's pretty doggone funny.

Got work today at Movie Mayhem. I'm guessing I must have mentioned that already about my being a Video Store Clerk. No wait now with my promotion I'm Video Rental Associate. Well on Thursdays and Saturdays (my working days) I shower and make myself all presentable but that is just not going to be possible today. There's just all kinds of things jammed into the shower stall. Two AC units and a mounted deer head with the fur all falling out and a few flat bicycle tires and some half-empty jugs of vinegar and wires of some sort all tangled together and some plastic bins filled with magazines and newspapers I salvaged from our neighbors' recycling bins. They never say anything when they see me going through their bins. Nice folks.

"Skeet Jeffcoat Deveaux get you're *ss out here!" Gamps shouts. It's early for Gamps to be up and early for shouting and all that which does not bode well for me I'll tell you what.

When I open the door and step out of the bathroom there's a blur in the corner of my vision and Gamps's cane wallops me in the side of the head. Everything flashes purple and silver and I hunch over shielding my head with my arms as the cane swings down on me again and again.

"Well mister you did it! You got an explanation for this!?"

"I'm sorry Gamps! I'm sorry! What did I do? I'm sorry! I'm sorry!" I don't know what's happening but I keep repeating these phrases hoping that one of them is the right thing to say the one that will make the beating stop.

Eventually Gamps let's up panting and mad as heck. When I open my eyes I see that the pull down was opened and the ladder is broken to bits and scattered on the ground. It smells awful just like I remember that incident with the dead squirrel and all our pine tree air fresheners which is something I will tell you about later if

I have not already done so. Got so many doggone things going on sometimes I can't keep my mind half straight.

"Well?" His chest is heaving and his eyes are all gray from the cataracts like an overcast sky inside him leaking out through his eyes. "I sure as h*ll didn't do this."

"I-I-I... I reckon it was me Gamps. Dang it I'm sorry." I tear up a bit. My face is hot and sore from where he struck me.

It was Iltday yesterday wasn't it?

I want to ask him but I got this feeling that if I do he'd just pop me one again upside the head. I never have a good recollection of Iltdays aside from the red. "Heck what're we gonna do now?"

"How many d*mn times did I tell you not to go up there? The sh*t I put up with with you. It's a curse a d*mned curse on my life. I don't know what to do with you."

"Sorry Gamps."

"I know you're sorry. Sorry and useless." He hobbles back a few steps and leans up against the cabinet with the elves. Out of breath. After a spell he calms down and the Iltday red flushing his face fades and he looks empty like the Saturday fish had nibbled on and sucked him lifeless. "I'll get it fixed up. Gamps'll handle it. Like he always does. What the h*ll got into you anyway?"

—*Don't tell him.*—

"I-I-I guess I don't remember going up there Gamps."

He sighs. "Welp. I'll get to it after I take you in to work. Jasper Deveaux can still be handy around the house when the situation calls for it." Limping away he shakes his head with disappointment.

"I'll-I'll get you some Calders."

"Best D*mn Cup Is *Every* Cup."

We eat our breakfast in the kitchen for once because Gamps is up early. Got bacon (Bubba Joe's) and Waffacombs Now With Superhex Syrup Pockets which has the clever slogan "Waffa Matta With You?" which I looked up in the dictionary and Waffa is not in there. Neither is Superhex. Also Gamps gets his Calders in him. Fact is Gamps is wearing what he had on Friday maybe because he fell asleep in the family room with the television on (a not-too-uncommon occurrence in our household). We got morning news on the little portable and look who it is it's Mark Morales local weatherman warning us that Danny is on its way crawling up the southeastern United States.

"Ought to strike sometime tonight" Gamps says. He's in a better mood now. Smiling at me and reaching across the table and patting my shoulder and saying how great the breakfast was and that I'd make one heck of a short-order cook.

"Heck Gamps it ain't no Hugo. Category 1 ain't nothing to worry about."

"Ain't even that anymore. Just a tropical mess. But best to get ready. Scout's motto: Be prepared. I'll stock up on water and canned goods. You'd better dig up the camping stove and kerosene tanks in case we need 'em."

"All right Gamps."

"You done with breakfast?"

"I reckon so." I could eat or not eat again a breakfast part two.

"All right. Turn this mess off and put on Kenny Rogers. That'll fix my mood."

I got to rummage. I won't lie it's a danged mess in here and I got piled up a lot of those "Achy Breaky Heart" mixes not properly finished ones and just as many audio recordings of *The Wizard of Oz*. Eventually I get it into the tape deck and when I click it on guess what comes on but "The Gambler" and Gamps starts tapping his foot to the fast-picking guitar at the beginning.

Kenny comes in singing and it's basically just about a couple of people talking about cards is what I can make out of it. Poker I imagine. The game Gamps plays at American Legion with all the other vets.

I go back down the hall past the pull down mess careful not to glance up into the hot dark of the attic then go on into my room because it's Saturday and that means work at Movie Mayhem. But oh heck did I shower yet?

Smell my pits.

Smell all right.

I slide some of the mattresses around in my room kind of puzzle-like you might call it like one of those sliding tile puzzles which I actually have somewhere in here in all this mess a Garfield and Odie one if I recollect correct. Then I pull out my polo shirt for work and behind it is a human foot pale as powder with Saturday-purple polish dotting its toenails. I stumble backwards calling out in surprise and accidentally knock over one of the mattresses and sprawl out on it landing on my behind. The foot and leg retract into the gray dark of the closet. With the blinding sunlight streaming in through the window I can't hardly see what's in the closet beyond. Should have struck on the lights but I wasn't thinking about human feet in my closet.

Thought I was alone.

In the other room I hear Gamps start singing along to Kenny. I ought to run run run and call Gamps in here or we could call Mr. Soon-To-Be-Mayor Lingdenberry or the police that Officer Marnie who interrogated me at the station. She was nice. She was the nice one. The Good Cop.

The clothes hanging up rustle and the hangers click together.

"Come out now you hear me?" I say. Whisper is more like it 'cause my throat is thick and I can't speak properly. Like I'm choking on something. Something painful.

Several shirts tumble onto the floor and some of the clothes part as if by a ghost. Then something beyond it slides down almost like something had been clinging to the back wall and the clothes push forward in a wave. A shape creeps towards me. Along the floor. Inching into the morning light slanting in through the narrow window. I see a foot there naked and pale as I'd never seen skin before. Looks like a child's foot it's so slender and small but the toes are too long and these toenails are different than the ones I saw previously. Banana yellow. Tuesday's color. The wrong doggone day.

The foot creeps forward blinding almost it's so white. And the leg is an unusual kind of appendage it is. It's it's it's. The muscles bulge in all the wrong ways and in places I've never seen before. Wrong. Wrong.

"Don't come nearer." Don't come nearer. Don't come don't come. No no.

—*Why not?*—

"Just don't." Don't don't don't. Please no.

Something else wrong with that leg. Its knees. Bending in backwards. One of them is. The other one bends the right way. Too many knees. Opposing each other. I don't see how don't see don't see don't look.

—*Open your eyes Skeet. I'm not going to hurt you.*—

"I just want my shirt and want to put it on and want to go to Movie Mayhem and work that's all I want."

—*Don't speak Skeet. Just think. We can talk like that. Your Gamps doesn't like you to talk to yourself. It disturbs him. Let's not disturb him.*—

"Yes Ma'am. I mean" Yes Ma'am. Okay Ma'am.

—*Good. Take your shirt and go. I won't hurt you.*—

Yes Ma'am.

The shirt lands in a bundle in the patch of light. Tossed there I don't know how by. But there it is. The leg withdraws the foot too with it disappearing back into the gray dimness of the closet. I scramble forward and grab the shirt and put it on over the other one the one with the kitten hanging on that says "Hang in There!" which is funny if you think about it.

—*What's funny Skeet?*—

I need my khakis Oh God Oh Jesus my khakis my my work khakis the pants the—

The khaki pants appear in the patch of light dangling there off the big toe of the foot. This isn't nice I don't want to touch it don't want to get any closer than I already am but I need my pants need my work khakis or Russell's going to have a fit. Don't want to get near those legs with the veins the veins blue and purple tangles of them underneath all that pale whiteness connecting all wrong veined in an unnatural way.

There's a laughing in my head. Soft and bright and high-pitched like a little girl's almost like Judy Garland's yet unlike hers not— don't think it stop Skeet—not really human.

—*Take the pants Skeet.*—

I can't move Ma'am.

—*Take them before your Gamps becomes distressed. That would be bad Skeet. Bad for everyone.*—

I close my eyes and reach forward slowly 'cause I don't want to see the thing there holding the pants out to me. My hand seems to reach across the world seems to reach over a bottomless abyss seems to reach to the moon and stars seems to reach forever—but then suddenly the fabric is in my clutching fingers and I yank the pants back and breathe out a sigh of relief.

Then something brushes up against my hand. Not warm not flesh warm but cool like the wormy soil under a rock after you flip it over in the garden.

The voice laughs in my head again as I scramble back and start retching.

—*That's no way to treat an old friend Skeet.*—

I'm sorry Ma'am.

—*Don't apologize. There's no need. I'm just having some fun with you. Do you remember the last time we had fun?*—

"The Gambler" has ended and I can hear the floor creaking as Gamps turns off the tape turns off the beginning of "Daytime Friends" and then shouts out to me to get my keister in gear.

—*Better listen to him. We'll see each other later.*—

Okay. Okay.

—*It's going to be a fun day Skeet.*—

I burst out of my room and slam the door shut and change out in the hallway looking at that mess from the pull down from where something crashed down from darkness above.

As we pull out of the driveway I watch the front door and scan the windows the window into the living room and the other one to the spare room where we store all kinds of things. Can't see anything moving around there. Then when we pass beyond our house I turn back and can just make out the narrow window to my bedroom the one that looks onto the side of Deidre Thomas's house. Nothing there either.

"What the High H*ll you gawping at?"

Nothing Gamps.

"You wanna answer me boy?"

"Yessir. Sorry sir. I wasn't staring at… at nothing Gamps."

"Gimme my coffee."

I hand over his mug with purple things swimming in it. Purple things which he sips right down like he can't see them like they don't exist. We don't have operational cupholders in the Hamtramck. Or rather we did have them until Gamps transformed them into loose-change pits to use for parking meters.

"I won't lie. You look spooked. And your pants are on back-wards."

I stare down at my pants. "Aw heck." I try to take them off and switch them around but my legs are too danged long too cramped in here.

Gamps starts laughing shaking his head. "I never." He pulls over on the side of the highway. "Run off to them trees and set them aright."

"Yuh-yessir."

I huff it a few yards into the pine woods just beyond Sumter Road and pop off my combat boots and shimmy out of my pants then get everything on right but as I'm buckling my cowboy belt I catch movement out of the corner of my eye and freeze. It's hot but there's a stiff breeze and the trees are creaking and their needly heads making a continuous shush like ocean surf. It was a planted forest and you can tell this Gamps told me because all the trees are in neat rows but huge too 'cause they were planted about a hundred years ago or more. Whoever did it might have included a bunch of different types of trees but they went with 100% pine so it's a kind of series of hallways of pine trees and if I move left or right I can glance down the next hallway over and when I do glance over something in the far distance ducks just out of view. A whitish shape tall and thin.

The horn honks.

Gamps is waving at me to hurry.

I run back to the truck glancing over my shoulder but there's no sign of that whiteness out in the woods.

"What the heck's gotten into you today?" Gamps asks me as we pull back onto the road.

"Thought I saw something out in those woods" I say watching down the lanes of pine as they blur past. Can't see anything in there but row after row always the same the ground matted in needles with little purple creatures squirming over them. Best to tell him everything I think. Best to say it all about how Iltday came and how maybe something came in from the attic. Come to think of it. Hadn't this thing come before? Can't rightly say.

"Gamps" I say. "Yesterday was Iltday—"

"Oh Kheeeerrrriiiist."

"—and I think we may be in trouble—"

"Not in the mood for this today."

"—and there was ghost feet—"

"Grab me a cigarette."

"—and the lady was talking inside my head."

Gamps glances over at me. "You done?"

I nod. "Yessir."

"All right well first off light me a cigarette like I done told you." I fish a cigarette out of the pack and start lighting it. Never actually smoked a cigarette even if I am twenty-one and a grown adult except for when I get a taste like this when I light it up for Gamps. If I'm honest I don't care for the taste much. "There's a good boy."

He takes the cigarette I hand him and the smoke dribbles off his lips and down through his beard along a yellow-stained path then disperses when he cracks open the window.

"Now. I got too much on my mind today what with the pull down that you broke and what's more this son of a hot wet b*tch of a hurricane creeping up our *sses. I don't got time in the day for… ghost feet and ladies talking inside my idiot grandson's head thank you very much. You hear me? You listening to me?"

I nod. "Yessir."

"Now I know I lost my temper this morning. I am a man fallible like all the rest. I try to be even-keeled Lord knows but sometimes… I don't know."

I nod though I don't know what he's getting at.

"What I'm saying is you need to quit it with the nonsense or I'm going to lose my f*cking mind. Lose it worse than you ever seen before."

I don't like the sound of that so I don't say anything else but I turn my eye on the rearview mirror and the woods on our right making sure nothing is following us but it's just the familiar country in the middle of morning. Hot as heck and the heat still building and nothing to see for miles around. Flat and without surprise.

The woods pull away from us and then there's farms for a mile and then the big doggone crucifix and iceberg church and the Willy Nilly's and Quick Change where Gamps gets the oil changed and their prices are pretty reasonable.

Well nothing could have followed us that fast for that far not a flock of flying monkeys nor anything else I could fathom. We stop at a traffic light before crossing the bridge and I turn for another glance at the road behind us just to make sure it's safe. The back of the Hamtramck is still full up with some of our Treasure Cruise finds and a few additions Gamps must have picked up the other day. Lightweight stuff. Stuff he could hoist with his bad leg and all. Half a side table and a wrought-iron bed frame and a light fixture and a big metal bucket with a hole in it but not too big a hole and a little glass-paneled house for storing plants in with a few of the glass panes shattered but fixable I suppose and a big swath of crumpled-up tarp and the limb of a mannequin pale and deformed and speckled green with mold in places and bent and bulging in ways you don't normally see on a mannequin.

I stare at the thing. Buried under the rest of Gamps's dumpster finds just a piece of it visible.

It doesn't move.

I turn to Gamps to say something but he doesn't pay me any heed. Just says "Real American City." Then "My *ss!" He has a chuckle and I try to join in but can't for the life of me understand what is funny and instead of speaking turn to look through the rear window into the bed of the truck into the complicated jigsaw of dumpster treasure and it's too confusing and I can't find what I was looking for can't find that pale moldy crook of flesh that hiding secret thing.

The truck stops in front of Movie Mayhem.

"Well what're you waiting for there Mr. Skeet?"

I don't see it back there anymore don't see the leg.

"Not to worry. You can help me unload after work."

Feeling disoriented. Dizzy. Might be sick. Might vomit if I move.

I don't open the door. Never open the door. That's right. I'd forgotten. Never open the door.

"Make sure to get us a movie today. What was it you were talking about renting the other day?"

"All right Gamps" I manage to say finally. "All right Gamps."

Overcoming that sick feeling I do open the truck door and get out and stand at the entrance of Movie Mayhem watching as Gamps's Hamtramck pulls away across the uneven broken parking lot and turning with squealing wheels onto West Main. Even with all the Saturday morning traffic you can hear the cicadas sawing away like millions of tiny chainsaws splitting torsos at least that's probably what Russell would say which is why I thought of it 'cause he's standing there when I turn and enter.

"Sup d*ckhead." He's got on another weird shirt black that says NIN on it and one of the Ns is backwards but that's an easy mistake to make done it tons of times. His face is bruised too. Right around the nose. Most likely from when his daddy Mr. Lingdenberry straightened him out. Or was it something else?

"A'ight Russell" I say just like how his daddy says it. I stand there a moment and then remember all about the big news. "I spoke with your daddy yesterday and he's given me a promotion to Video Rental Associate which is higher up than Video Store Clerk."

"Oh" he says. I can't make out his eyes beyond the shine of his glasses.

"That's right."

"Oh. God. Jesus. I'm sorry. Video Rental Associate Deveaux. Or is it Video Rental Associate Jeffcoat Deveaux?"

"Just Skeet is fine with me Russell but we are going to have to make some changes around here now that I'm promoted."

"Well all right." He smiles. "All right. I'm on board with that."

"First—"

"Wait wait. I know. Let's pipe musicals and other gay sh*t twenty-four seven and all staff have to wear *Wizard of Oz* costumes."

"That's not a half-bad idea."

"How about you get your r*tarded head out of you're *ss and get the drive-by box?"

He's not supposed to use that word. I heard his daddy chew him out a number of times when he heard Russell say it. Mrs. Kelly from All-Star Class said it was a bad word and only bad people used it. Now that I'm his superior at Movie Mayhem I reckon I ought to set him straight but while I'm thinking what to say Russell pipes up. "On the double douchebag!"

Come to think of it Mr. Lingdenberry didn't go over with me any changes in duties following my promotion so I guess getting the drive-by box is still part of the job. Well I reckon we will work everything out eventually. Probably the back office will be mine and I can have Burger Braggers delivered at lunch and we can add the appropriate colors to the shift calendar.

I go around the counter to clock in and then as I get the keys I hear footsteps behind me pounding against the carpet then Russell's got hold of me yanking my boxer shorts up from the rear and I yell and thrash and then whip around and swing at his stupid laughing face but he dodges out of the way and I fall over from the momentum of the punch. Russell scampers away laughing and I get up pulling the painful wedgie out of my butt crack.

"I'm gonna get you!" I say getting my pants back in place.

"Bring it big boy."

"I ought to. I ought to… sit on you. Ought to make you my footstool. Ought to make you squirm under me."

"That's for popping me last Thursday bee-hatch. Nice shiner by the way. Was that my work?"

I storm out of there out of the cool of the AC and into the wall of broiling humidity. There's waves of heat washing off the blacktop of the shopping center parking lot hot enough to make the Burger Braggers all distorted and wavy and though the sky is purple swimming in blue I remember that a hurricane's coming and for some reason Hurricane Danny reminds me about what happened this morning with the foot in my room and the white blur in the woods and then the moldy skin in the bed of the pickup. There were hurricanes before if I'm not mistaken. Storms and doors. The two words fit together for some reason in my mind.

In *The Wizard of Oz* at the end of the movie Dorothy taps her ruby slippers and then wakes up as if from a dream back in Kansas with all her family and the farmhands gathered around her bed and it turns out that they had all dressed up as the Lion and the Tin Man and the Scarecrow in I guess a dream or I guess not. You can't quite tell at the end of the movie if I'm honest about it and that's how I feel right now like I'm in some kind of land between dreaming and waking 'cause I saw the foot and I heard the voice talking to me and saw something in the woods something pale and inhuman something that could make me sweat even without all this heat.

"What took you so long?" Russell asks.

"Nothing." I bring the cart of movies into the back and get to rewinding them. The horror ones I try not to look at the covers of them. *Videodrome* and *Pet Sematary* and *My Bloody Valentine* and *Night of the Demons*. Why do people watch this stuff?

"I'm going out back for a smoke" Russell calls to me. "Beep me if my dad shows up."

I pop in a tape and slam the machine closed. It whirs and I place my hand on it watching the thickness of tape move from one reel to the other and my hand vibrating all the while. This is the moment I love at work. The feeling of rewinding a tape to the beginning. The act of it. Undoing what you saw or what you did. I dream about it sometimes long dreams that stretch on forever me sitting in a dark room beside a mountain of videotapes and popping them in one by one. We have a sign asking people to "Be Kind Rewind" of course but truthfully I don't want anyone to rewind their tapes 'cause I want to do it myself. When they get all the DVDs in and start dumping the VHS tapes in the dumpster out back and with them the VCRs and Lumovox 1-Way VHS Rewinders I reckon I will take every one and build a warehouse beyond our home stretching out into the unused farmland and will reconstruct this place as it is at this very moment. We got all that danged shelving anyway. Maybe no one will want the videos anymore because DVDs have taken over but that's okay with me. Probably Deidre Thomas and Jim Byrd will come and I will even let Russell in if he wants to remember what it used to look like in the place where he worked for so many years. Maybe everyone will come and they will say "You were right Skeet. We shouldn't have made DVDs and shouldn't have made that horrible horrible mistake. Look what DVDs have done to us! Look what we've become as a result." With their skin rotting and their eyes melting out like sugary icing.

—*Skeet. Close your eyes.*—

The rewinder clicks to a stop and I stare down at it confusedly. "What?" I ask it.

—*I'm here. Close your eyes. I want to show you something.*—

I close my eyes but the instant that darkness settles over me another pair of eyes opens up upon a world cast in Iltday red the eyes not mine not positioned in the usual place but removed from the side of my head. I... it's hard to explain how but the eyes are somewhere else and I can feel the heat and the humidity pressing down on me and my stomach is clenched tight and painful and so so so hungry as if I hadn't eaten in days and days and in front of me is the dumpster where all those VHS tapes will be dumped when the DVD truck arrives and I can smell the sharp sting of cigarette smoke wafting across my nose and just beyond the edge of the dumpster just peeking around the corner I see Russell in his baggy black t-shirt and baggy jeans his hair long and stringy standing there leaning against the brick wall and staring off into the empty back lot the backs of other stores with dumpsters and nondescript metal doors and no windows no windows anywhere but stretching up beyond everything and stabbing the sky the pine tree eternity of Pinehouse.

—*You see him. See him. What shall I do Skeet? What shall I do? It's almost time you know.*—

I open my eyes and stagger backwards overturning the cart of VHS tapes which spill every which way and I crush a couple of the cases under my butt then scramble to my feet and shouting and cussing sprint towards the other end of the store back through the storeroom then burst through the back door out into the heat and grab Russell by the collar of his shirt.

"What the f*ck?!"

His cigarette explodes in a cloud of sparks but I got him I got him I got him and yank him back into the hallway.

"F*cking dipsh*t! What's with you?"

Before the door slams shut I catch sight of something moving out there but the door closes too quick. I'm not certain. Not certain of anything.

Russell's hands are on me. "You ripped my shirt f*ckhead!" I did hear a rip come to think of it a rip that I had tried not to hear because I thought I-I-I feared it was some *other* sound not of clothes tearing but a sound from one of Russell's horror movies.

"Russell" I say trying to catch my breath. "It's… all right. You're… all right. Something was… out… there."

Staring at me he gives an exasperated sigh.

—*I'm* still *here Skeet. I'm* still *here.*—

There's a scratch at the door. A long scratch moving from the handle down to the bottom where the daylight streams in and you can see something there a thin shadow. Then the shadow disappears and the scratch starts again moving from the top down. It gives me the shivers hearing that sound that metallic scratching.

"What is that?" Russell asks.

He can hear it.

That's good.

—*Open the door for me Skeet.*—

"Go away!" I shout.

The scratching stops suddenly and after several seconds Russell pushes past me and though I try to stop him he shoves me again and then opens the door. I hold my breath looking past him into the back lot waiting for something to happen. I don't know what. The hot air rushes in with the sunlight. You can hear the traffic and cicadas. Can see from the swaying pines and skittering parking lot refuse how windy it's getting.

But nothing happens. And when I blink against the sunlight the only red I see now is the light shining through my eyelids.

Nothing happens the rest of that morning. The two of us are silent going about our duties. Russell notices the crushed cassette cases but doesn't say anything just takes the sleeves out and slips them and the tapes into new cases. Even shelves them for me. Normally he would probably rail into me for something like that happening. Damage to store property his daddy's store and his too by rights at least eventually. He'll see it change through to DVDs and MCTs and UFEs and whatever other nonsense they come up with.

No customers all morning. We go several hours before Russell realizes there isn't a movie playing on the store system. He pops in *Something About Mary* which is that raucous comedy I may have mentioned to you before and not one of his typical horror movies. He puts on a blue polo shirt over his NIN t-shirt so you can't see the rip along the shoulder even though you can still kind of tell there's something wrong 'cause the black collar is all skewed.

Everything feels wrong today. Probably on account of Iltday coming yesterday. The day feels sandwiched and broken.

It's almost lunchtime when he finally asks me "Skeet what was out there? A bobcat? Coyote?"

"I don't know what. But. I know you were in danger."

"How did you know? You see it slip around back or something?"

I shrug my shoulders.

"What the h*ll kinda answer is that? I'm talking to you civilly. Least you could do is answer." He has a cigarette out. Tapping it against the counter then flipping it in his fingers and tapping it some more which is supposed to pack the tobacco and make it a better smoking experience according to Russell. He doesn't sound as peppy as he usually does nor as ready to fight me or pick on me. It's strange having a friend that wants to fight all the time but Gamps can be like that too I guess.

"What's it matter anyway? You heard something was out there Russell?"

A car pulls up outside and our conversation ends 'cause it's a particular car a cherry-red Romulus convertible with the top pulled down and Mr. Lingdenberry's head sticking out of it with some mirror shades on and his pleased expression 'cause Mr. Lingdenberry always seems like he's having a good time or just had a good time or maybe is right on the verge of it.

Russell hides the cigarette behind the counter and straightens up a bit. I stop shelving and watch Mr. Lingdenberry as he hops out of the car wondering if I should warn him about... what? A foot with painted toenails? Moldy skin? A storm? Not sure exactly.

He pauses and goes to greet the mailwoman who just pulled up too and he takes the mail from her and seems ready to have a nice long chat the way he looks sometimes the way his long body settles against the side of the mail truck. Every second I stare out into the heat is like pinpricks inside me up and down my insides. He's leaning in the window of the mail truck and gesturing and laughing and getting her laughing as well while I scan the parking lot scouting for anything unusual.

Didn't even realize I had been shelving videos all this time. And making a mess of things from the looks of it. Mixing Horror movies in with the Children's section.

Christ Almighty Skeet Jeffcoat Deveaux what were you thinking?

I make a frantic search through the shelves looking for horror stickers on the spines of the cases but then the voice comes to me again and my vision grows swimmy and fuzzy and

—*Skeet look out the window I'm still here. I'm with you.*—

I look up and my eyes dance across the glass wall of Movie Mayhem like one of those *Where's Waldo?* books eyes darting this way and that to the parking lot beyond and the lines of fast-food restaurants along the road then to the mail truck and Mr. Lingdenberry who's leaning into the window of the truck and smiling and the mailwoman is smiling too but in a different way in the way we are supposed to use when we really actually want someone to go away and that was actually covered in our All-Star Class with Mrs. Kelly who said that sometimes people might smile at us but what the smile really means is stop touching me and please give me more than three feet of space. I remember after having that lesson walking around at home and talking with various things in the house and using a yardstick and finding that boy howdy I had definitely been talking too close to people just Like Mr. Lingdenberry is now with the mailwoman.

—*Is that Mr. Lingdenberry? Yes it is isn't it?*—

I see it now.

A foot. White and moldy with toenails painted in sky blue. Wednesday blue. No. No. Not that color. Not my favorite. Not the happy color. It's pressed against the back side of the drive-by box. The foot is reaching just above the bottom ledge of the window so I can't see what all it's attached to.

And it's not exactly a foot. Must've been that I'd seen it wrong before and mistaken it for a foot or couldn't decide what else it could've been and so thought of it as a foot. But not now. Now I see clearly it thrumming its toes or digits or whatever against the gray-green metal surface of the box I realize it's not a foot at all but maybe a strangely shaped hand a hand with too-short fingers and a too-long palm. But feminine. No doubt. Not just 'cause the nails are painted but also 'cause there's a delicacy to them almost dainty like a girl's dollhouse or Deidre Thomas's hands and the way she paints her nails so precisely like maybe she had fairies come out and do it for her or maybe her nails were Made in China or I don't know what but this foot-thing is not a him or a he or a his.

"No no no." I turn towards Russell and say "You see it? You see it?" but when I turn back again the foot has slid down out of visibility invisible gone.

—*No Skeet I'm still here. I wouldn't leave you but I want him I do. I need him for the symmetry of the thing. For aesthetic reasons. Don't you want me to have him?*—

"Help me neaten up back here Skeet." I can hear Russell start tidying up but I can't rip my eyes from the scene can't look anywhere else something pale barely cresting over the ledge of the window but then the door dings open and Mr. Lingdenberry is standing in the entry the AC sucking out round him into the heat and I'm staring out at nothing.

"Look alive there Skeet."

I straighten up. A "Yessir" comes out.

"That's more like it. Look at you two." He shakes his head and I can't tell if it's a happy moment a pleased happiness for him or not. He looks happy but like he's sucking on and savoring a sour candy. "How's business? How many customers this morning?"

"Zip." That's Russell. I wouldn't use that word talking to my boss Mr. Lingdenberry and future Pinehouse Mayor at that.

I look from Russell to his father and back as their conversation flows in and out through my head like water you can't catch hold of it nothing at all to show for the effort but just the wet trail where it was and a hairy mucky algae slime from all the water flowing over it time and again.

Scratch scratch scratch.

—Let me in Skeet. Let me show you what fun we can have with them.—

"Excuse me y'all" I say because speaking makes the voice stop and the scratching and I hear something scuttling and dragging away along the length of the store outside as if it were something with many legs most of them agile but one of them gimp.

They both turn toward me and I can see that they were arguing but I can't imagine what about.

"I-I need to say…"

"Speak up Skeet." It's the Future Mayor Lingdenberry.

"I just gotta say something which is which is which is… don't go out there sir. And you neither Russell. Don't go out to the parking lot. There's something waiting out there for us."

"What? You saw the coyote or whatever come back?" From behind the counter Russell cranes his neck to peer out the store window. I don't know why he keeps talking about coyotes. Never said nothing about danged coyotes. "I don't see jack sh*t."

Mr. Lingdenberry disregards the parking lot and continues to scrutinize me. "You all right there Skeet? Look a bit pale and perspiring."

I shake my head. "Nosir. Nosir I ain't."

He smiles. "I don't make you nervous do I?"

"Nosir. It ain't that. It's just... just that. Something been following me. All morning. And I'm getting scared about it." My throat chokes up with tears and my eyes start leaking just a bit. Russell's going to let me have it good for this going to let me suffer for these tears.

"Is that so?" He turns and walks back towards the door. "Not a danged thing out there."

"Yeah there ain't no coyote. Skeet's spooked is all."

"It ain't a coyote so shut up about it!" I don't know why I'm yelling at Russell. "Why I'll bet it-it's something sprung out of Iltday."

"Woah Nellie" Russell says under his breath.

"Sprung out of... what now? What was that you said?" Mr. Lingdenberry is close enough to me now that I can look him eye to eye man to man and water my eyes do from the sting of his cologne which is so strong and thick it's like an invisible layer of skin surrounding him and swallowing me up.

"I said it—"

—She *Skeet*. She. *But why would you tell them about me?*—

"She. She sprung from Iltday. I've known it since this morning 'cause it was just Ilteve yesterday or I guess two days ago now and I don't know what She wants but trouble probably. Trouble."

Russell starts singing "We're Off to See the Wizard!"

"Can it Russell! Skeet?" He's lowered his voice and is so close now we're practically one flesh me and the future mayor. "Did your granddad talk to you about those signs?"

My head moves in a way neither a nod nor a shake and I say some kind of a a a nonwordthing.

"If you're feeling guilty about something then you can tell me. I won't make you feel ashamed for it. You know me. I'm a forgiving man."

"Nosir. I mean yessir. Gamps was all upset about those By His Bootstraps signs and so he drove me around town and we picked up a pretty sizable stash of them."

He puts his hands on my shoulders firm a firmness you couldn't budge your way out of. "I see. You did right to tell me Skeet. To tell your boss. Your... your friend. Do you consider me your friend?"

I look down. My combat boots. Awfully scuffed. And his shiny loafers about as big and boat-like as mine. "I don't know sir."

"Well I believe you are. I consider you to be my friend. Good friends. You and me. Forget all this Movie Mayhem nonsense who is whose boss etc. we're talking man to man now and I'm telling you you're my friend and especially for working up the courage to tell me you took those signs. Now where'd you put 'em at Skeet? I'm a man who wants to set things right in the community. That's why I'm running for mayor in the first place."

"In the in the tobacco shed."

"Which is where now? Think."

"Near our house. It is. In the woods there." I look up at him. "Pine woods on top of a hill."

"That's more like it." He smiles. I never noticed before how many fillings he's got in there so many that there's more darkness than teeth.

"Now listen here." He turns back to Russell. "We gonna close early today. Shutter up these windows so as not to suffer any wind damage. Danny's likely to be nothing more than a whimper but they're saying conditions are ripe for tornadoes. And no one's gonna be out renting movies in this mess."

Mr. Lingdenberry is already over talking with Russell and they forgot about me standing over here and what was it anyway I'd had to tell them? About. About. About that foot that paleness and manicured toes joints bending wrong and moldering skin.

His business concluded Mr. Lingdenberry heads to the door. Russell's sulking like always when his father comes. I meet Mayor Bossman Lingdenberry at the doorway and block his path. "You can't go sir."

"Outta my way Skeet." He smiles. Everything is just a smile. That could be a new *Wizard of Oz* song.

"I gotta go first."

"Well on with you then boy."

I step outside into the heat. It's like stepping through a stickiness a clinging film of salt sweat. And look around at all the—

for the—

no one—

there.

Nothing.

Mr. Lingdenberry is breathing down my neck. "All clear Skeet Jeffcoat?"

"Yessir. I reckon so sir." Can't stop staring at his shoes his shiny brown shoes. Big as canoes.

His hand finds my shoulder. Just the two of us out here alone now. "I ever told you I knew your mother?"

"Nosir."

"Hired her on when I used to manage the Willy Nilly's. Before Movie Mayhem came along. She was having some trouble and I thought I'd help her out. Amazing resilient lady if I do say so myself. Pretty girl but had her demons. Believe you me all the pretty ones have demons." He sighs. "A bad business."

"Yessir." He's not talking about Movie Mayhem when he says a bad business.

"I take care of you don't I? You and Gamps?"

"Yessir."

Talking about what happened at the other house the white one with the blue door. Talking about what I didn't see. Talking about what I heard about how they found her. And that poor poor Skeet. Not me but another one. Another Skeet. Found alone staring in the bedroom at the running splatter over the head of the bed and a feces stink and blood burnt and a fly jittering out of her mouth. And a shotgun.

Not talking about Movie Mayhem at all.

His hand leaves my shoulder. Up and off.

Hours go by and no more voices. I don't risk going out to get my Burger Braggers but Russell isn't afraid so he drives out and picks up some bacon cheeseburgers from Kirby's which are pretty tasty actually but Russell doesn't know if the bacon is Bubba Joe's

(Hear That Sizzle) Ultra Thick Cut Bacon or not. No one comes in all day and Russell says I ought to go on home.

Still got an hour and a half left over before Gamps comes to collect me and he doesn't pick up when I call. Still it's probably safe probably I had just imagined the voices and everything so I head on out into the heat and I haven't reached the end of the parking lot before I'm soaked with sweat and need to escape back indoors somewhere and so I duck inside a convenience store the air all chilled and delightful. You can smell all the chocolate and candy from inside their wrappers and the motor oil in the aisle over and all the dead reeking things stuffed in the walls. I greet the plump cashier woman with spiked dark-red hair although she doesn't notice me on account of her reading one of those books with a burly long-haired half-naked man on the front. Fabio they call him. Wander down the aisles deciding what all I should get from about a thousand different candy bar options—light and dark chocolate pieces nuts king-sized everything crawling with purple fish the words all twisted and contorted and squirming like maggots just like on Gamps's Brweestr the other night. Can't read any of these darn candy bar names except for one in a dark-red package called Iltday (now with long leg painted toenails!).

The door dings again while my mind candy-swims and I grab the red-wrapped chocolate bar and then from the refrigerator get a cold beverage the radioactive green of Atomic Fizz Neon Lime Flavor (Fear the Fizz) but the letters of the label are all swirled out of place too.

When I go up to the counter to pay wouldn't you know it but the cashier lady has disappeared. There's her Fabio book lying on the floor behind the counter and below the cigarette display case I see a leg with a sneaker on it squeaking and juddering as it drags across the ground and out of view. Can hear something else too the sound of cracking and splitting and ripping. A red mist bursts out suddenly spraying the linoleum and the plastic shield over the cigarettes.

"M-ma'am?" I say.

—*Yes Skeet?*—

I blink and in a flash of red I'm somewhere else in some other part of the convenience store down behind the counter I think and there are two fat legs stuffing into my mouth and I feel all my teeth grinding on bone and sinew and blood gushing down filling up the honeycombed pockets inside my gullet the way syrup fills up those Superhex Syrup Pockets on a Waffacomb.

Then just as quickly I'm standing back in my combat boots and my hand shaking I drop the money on the counter and get the heck out of there back out into the heat back away from the entrance. But through the darkened glass I can just make out a pale tangle of limbs slipping over the top of the counter and vanishing down toward the bathroom corridor and back rooms. I drop my candy bar and soda into the plastic bag I got with my movie in it (The No Place Like Home No Place Like Home No Place Like Home movie in case you were wondering) and hightail it through the parking lot and down the sidewalk along West Main which is always West for some reason. Seem to remember there used to be an East Main a long time back but the road got all tore up and flooded. Completely wrecked by a storm. Now there's just West Main. A West without an East and no symmetry.

Cars honking.

Someone hollers.

The world seems slow-moving and gigantic like I'm a bit of food passing down its massive purple-specked throat.

—Don't run Skeet. It's difficult for me to follow. Ever since you struck me with that hammer. But don't worry. I forgive you. And I'll be in fine form again once the storm is here.—

Many stumbling blocks later I stop and fall onto a bench and look down the sidewalk towards the convenience store. Can still see the sign from here:

Main Depot
Unleaded $0.95
Premium $1.10

Try talking to the voice. What do you want? What do you want? What hammer?

No response.

I outran Her I reckon.

I open my chocolate bar. It's a gooey mess now but still tastes pretty good and gets my shaking fingers and mouth all chocolatey smearing all over the bottle of Atomic Fizz Neon Lime Flavor I'd purchased with it. I try to speak try to talk about what just happened back there but nothing makes sense. I couldn't have just seen that. Must have been one of Russell's horror movies flaring up inside my brain.

My sweaty chocolatey fingers can't get the cap off the drink. It's no wonder I think looking at my hands. My fingers are too big and not designed for this little bottle. Dang it dang it! If I can't get this opened God knows what's going to happen. I need to do it I just need to.

I set it down and stand up and walk off then turn around and run back at the bottle and rip the top off grunting and scared and spilling soda all over me. I sip it judicious-like 'cause it's got to last the three miles home and I don't want to dehydrate or nothing like that.

I sit back down and breathe.

Not much shade out here on the sidewalk nowhere to hide from the sun but I don't want to move anyway. My legs are weak and not working properly. I'm panting and can't breathe. Heart racing. I need to. Need to do something. Calm down Skeet. Calm down.

Everyone Knows.

Everyone Knows You.

Everyone Knows Skeet Jeffcoat Deveaux.

Then I remember I'd seen something like that before. Two years ago right after Iltday had come I had walked down to the Country Store and had taken a shortcut through the farm behind our house and Mr. Lyles came out on his front porch yelling at me to "Get the h*ll off my prop'ty!" But what he didn't know was that something was creeping along the wraparound porch and slipping into the open door behind him. And later after I had reached the Country Store and was getting my snacks and Atomic Fizz Neon Lime Flavor I blinked and saw Mr. Lyles's bottom half getting stuffed into my mouth.

I breathe at last.

Smack my legs.

Make myself stand.

Crane my neck to see the entrance of the convenience store. Someone pulled up there. Pumping gas. I ought to go there and tell them not to go in but as I am watching the man finishes up and drives off in his truck.

I start moving. Slow at first and glancing over my shoulder. Then I pick up speed. Can sense something moving through the alleys behind the stores—the tobacco shop and West Main Pawn and Cash 4 Gold. I can feel myself moving back there. Creeping then skittering then creeping. Whenever I blink my eyes I glimpse red. A red world and my eyes are angled close to the ground eyes that see differently hungrily everything more focused and defined. When I blink I'm no longer inside myself no longer inside Skeet Jeffcoat Deveaux.

Don't blink. Don't see out of Her eyes. Don't hear out of Her ears. Don't feel the creaking of all those joints. Don't feel fluids sloshing inside Her body. Don't feel the quick movements of my scuttling legs and the one dragging gimp one.

My eyes are painful dry about the time I reach the bridge and run blundering out through traffic so I can get to the side opposite of EAT in case the thing following me should think to run in there and mess with the girl my best friend and neighbor Deidre Thomas. I know that whatever happens I cannot let that come to be cannot let this thing know about her.

Got to keep Deidre Thomas out of my mind. I won't think about her won't think about Deidre Thomas and how she touched my hand once or twice or heck who knows how many times. Don't think. Just gotta move gotta get home get home safe and no one else hurt and get this thing back in the attic quick-like.

At the Welcome to Pinehouse Pop. 6305 Real American City 1992! sign I'm panting but relieved and for good measure say "Real American City My *ss!" but it's not so funny without Gamps here and with whatever it is out there following me. And that Pop. 6305 it's not accurate anymore because I swear someone just—

A car honks. "Hey Skeet!"

Russell's voice. He's pulled up behind me.

"Get in." He's not smiling at me. In all my rush I didn't notice the wind and the way the clouds are piling up to the south and tumbling over one another with a darkness to them. Lightning arcs back and forth across the face of the mass like flickering purple smiles. He's smoking. Russell is. His polo shirt's off and he's back in his ripped NIN shirt and the letters are even more jumbled and backwards than usual. AC gusting out with the smell of burning tobacco and noise like machines clashing together and someone screaming.

"You're sopping wet dude." He's got to shout a bit over the music.

I look down at my shirt and see chocolate stains and practically every inch dark with sweat.

"Come on. Get in." He puts the car in park and leans across and opens the door. It's his daddy's old maroon Belleville.

I can't move for some reason.

"You want a ride home or not?"

I nod.

"Well come on then."

I climb in and buckle up and clutch onto my plastic bag.

"I need to get home quick Russell. I'm in some trouble. Some bad bad trouble."

He tosses me a napkin from an old takeout bag in the map holder. "You look like you massacred the Easter Bunny."

I wipe my mouth with it and for a moment it seems like the chocolate I just wiped off is red like maybe there's blood smeared all over my face. I can taste the metal of it.

"You live out on Sumter Road right?" Russell asks. He doesn't see the blood. Doesn't notice. And when I look again at the napkin it's just chocolate. I lick it a bit. Tastes like chocolate. "Gross man. Here." He hands me the greasy old takeout bag and I dump the napkin in it.

"It's this way right?" he says pointing down the highway.

That's when the car lurches and the trunk pops open.

"What the h*ll?"

"Drive Russell!" I try to move the transmission into D like I'd seen Gamps do a zillion times and like I did once back when Ms. Elsworth was alive and I creamed her mailbox by accident before she was horribly murdered is how the police put it to me during our little interrogation. The transmission grinds and Russell slaps my hand away and opens the car door and steps out. I turn and watch him walk towards the back.

The trunk is bobbing up and down then slams shut before Russell gets back there and he pauses a moment before continuing on.

"Come back Russell!"

Cigarette dangling from his lips he ignores me and rounds the back of the car. I can hear him trying the trunk latch. He cusses. Russell does cuss from time to time but I guess you know that by now. Even I cuss sometimes though Lord knows I try not to. Gumma taught me better. Don't cuss. Don't kill. Yessir. Yes Ma'am. Open doors for ladies. Do my Skeet Jeffcoat best. Taught me all that.

I hold my breath and close my eyes not even knowing what I'm doing what I'm trying to accomplish but everything's dark and muffled (the screams and pounding of the music are quieter now but still close) and I taste blood and I know what I've done I know I've entered into Her. Then I hear the trunk latch jiggling and it's real loud now right up against my head. Almost like I'm in the danged trunk.

I open my eyes and see Russell returning to the front of the car. He climbs in. "D*mned thing shut itself. Jammed shut." He glances over at me.

"It's in there" I tell him.

—*Shhh Skeet you'll spoil the surprise.*—

"What are you talking about?" he asks pulling onto the road. He turns down the screams and guitar thrashing on the stereo. To hear me better. Or maybe to hear what's in the trunk.

"The thing is in your trunk."

He laughs. "What? Your bobcatoyote?"

I nod. No time to explain it's not a coyote or whatever it is he's thinking. "Been following me. It ate the cashier at the Main Depot." Tears are streaming down my cheeks now. Oh man. Russell's never going to let me live this down.

"It… ate a cashier? What are you saying exactly?" Driving. Checking mirrors. Glancing over at me.

I start blubbering don't know what the heck I'm saying.

"Dude get a grip."

"You gotta listen to me! It's in there! It's in the trunk! And it ate someone that cashier lady at the Main Depot."

"Yeah I heard you." He laughs uncomfortable-like. "I heard you. Just calm down will you? Listen to me all right?"

I wipe my eyes and nose. It feels like I'm pushing some massive weight back up inside myself but I calm down after a minute or so. Farms are sweeping past us. Blurred by my teary vision.

"You all right man?"

I nod. "Yeah I reckon so."

"You're seeing sh*t. Hallucinating. Like in a dream you know?"

"I-I-I guess so."

"You ought to see a doctor man. Keep an eye on the road will you? Tell me where I need to turn?"

"Okay. Okay. Okey dokey. It's Sumter Road. My name's Skeet Jeffcoat Deveaux. I'm twenty-one years old. I live at 512 Sumter Road and our phone number's 803-555-6713—"

"All right all right I got it. I've heard the spiel before."

The back of the car lurches and both Russell and I glance to the rear.

"Sh*t." Russell turns back to the road. "Must've hit something."

I keep staring back there not at the road behind us but at the back seat. The leather's worn. Ripped in one place.

"Anyway I was talking to my dad talking about how you were going off the rails today."

"Huh?" I turn towards him.

He adjusts his glasses. Can't see his eyes. "Hear me out. You gotta go to the doctor. Get checked out. Maybe they can help you. Maybe… maybe your cancer came back or something. Dad's gonna talk to your grandfather about it. In the meantime we can't have you at the store being a liability."

"Wait now. What does that mean?"

"If you were to act how you were today around customers freaking people out we could get into a situation Skeet. Struggling enough as it is with the Videopolis in town that we can't afford to scare off any of our customers. So what I mean is… is that you can't come back to work dude."

"What are you saying?"

"Christ man. You're fired." He sounds concerned but he's smiling a little too. Smiling like his daddy like he's about to have a real good time.

"You can't do this to me. You can't Russell. You just can't. I'm Video Rental Associate Skeet Jeffcoat Deveaux. Everyone Knows That. Everyone Knows Me. What will I do Thursdays and Saturdays? How will I watch my *Wizard of Oz*?" More tears are streaming down my face and I can't see anything through the blur. "What's this doggone garbage truck music anyway?" I smack my palm into his stereo and the music—if you want to call it that and I don't thank you very much—cuts off and the disc in the CD player makes a continuous and sick whirring. Not the good kind of sick either. There's a button dangling there and the face of the player is sunken into the console.

"The f*ck dude!"

Something shakes in the back of the car and we both turn towards the backseat then I close my eyes and feel the dark heat of the trunk of the car and listen to the sloshing of liquid inside me and how cramped and folded up I am and how my legs are squeezed together pressing up against—

THUD!

The back seat crashes down and a cluster of pale limbs bursts out of it. Russell screams and the things flood into the front of the car and seize hold of him and the vehicle jerks left careening off the road and leaping across the drainage ditch into a lane of pine. The leg things claw into Russell's flesh and I try to rip them away from his face and neck and arms and chest and whatnot but their hold is too tight.

Then we crash.

When I come to I seem to be tangled in ropes of light. Kind of beautiful actually. Glistening and shimmering.

Takes a moment for me to realize I'm covered in tiny gems of glass which sparkle in the light filtering down through the needly canopy. The wind has picked up. Hot and uncomfortable. Branches swaying. Creaking. The windshield is sagging inward and milky-looking. I reach out for Russell but the driver's seat is empty. All that's left of him is a shoe a black-and-white cross trainer on the floorboard. The backseat's empty too and you can see clear through into his trunk and how the lid is open back there and a squirrel has hopped inside to investigate.

A sound catches my ear.

A moaning.

I unbuckle my seatbelt and try the door. Jammed. I kick at it and ram up against it till it squeaks open and I tumble out onto the forest floor. When I blink and everything turns red through Her eyes I catch a glimpse of something wet and glistening in the pine needles and smelling of blood.

I hurry around the smashed-in and steaming front end where the car crumpled around the trunk of a big pine tree and there I find Russell. It was like how it was with Ms. Elsworth. The dismemberment I mean. The image of her legless body squirming across the kitchen floor flashes into my mind almost as if I had been there years ago and had witnessed the murder—or had committed it myself—a memory of that day when I had returned from the Country Store and stopped off to help her do some weeding. And while I was squatting there in the dirt she went on into the kitchen to feed her cat. She started screaming and I should have run in and helped but I couldn't couldn't couldn't move could barely breathe but when at last control returned to my body I ran home and was sick in the backyard.

There's not much left of Russell not much but his torso and head and half a leg and he's gawping at me and wriggling forward inching forward a kind of human-turned-maggot. His glasses are cracked and like bug eyes.

"Russell! Wh-what's happened?"

This horrible wailing creaks out of his mouth. It was the same sound Ms. Elsworth made too God rest her soul. The sound fills the woods and mingles with the wind and it seems to be part of the pine coming from the trees wavering as they rock and bend under the coming waves of the storm.

I heard once that arms and legs and whatnot could be reattached so thinking fast I ask him "Where are your arms at?" We could collect them and I could probably carry him to the hospital and get him all fixed up. He would likely need new glasses and his NIN shirt is ripped to shreds now but his limbs could be reattached for sure. It would be like re-stuffing the "If I Only Had A Brain" Scarecrow. Can't remember how many times they had to do that in the movie.

Still wailing he starts to slide backwards and I see that one of those pale limbs has latched onto the stump of his leg.

"I got you buddy." I leap towards him and grab hold of his long greasy hair and shirt and try to pull him free but the thing has a more solid grip and shirt and hair slip out of my hands and Russell whips around the corner of the car. I hear the shuffle of pine needles. Then something pops and snaps and the wailing becomes wet and garbled.

I turn away. Wide-eyed. 'Cause if I close them if I shut my eyes I'll see it I'll see what's happening to Russell I'll taste it and feel the hot pulsing textures of it. I want to help him want to put a stop to all this mess but I can't bring myself to do it. My legs move on their own and I huff it the heck out of there.

At home I slam the door shut panting and bleary-eyed. I'm dizzy and the world's tilting but I manage to lock the doors front and back dead bolt and all and go from room to room checking the windows. Gamps is in bed with the Happy Value Shopping on and shouts out to me about what all the commotion is all the stomping around and why am I home early from work.

What can I tell him? I told Russell and Mr. Lingdenberry the truth and they didn't listen. Gamps knows me better but I guess it won't make a difference.

"Skeet Jeffcoat you are a right mess just look at you soaked to the bone and pine straw in your hair and is that mud or chocolate on your face?" He's been smoking in here though he says he's not supposed to that Gumma would have had a fit if he smoked a cigarette in this household.

"Chocolate sir."

"Should've figured. Been a while since I caught you eating mud." He turns back to the Happy Value Shopping. "What's got you so spooked?"

"You wouldn't believe me."

He chuckles. "Probably right about that. Now this here looks promising."

On the TV set there is an old-timey diner table jukebox just like they got at EAT going for $49.99 but I can't focus on that right now.

"Gamps. I'm… in trouble. Two are dead. Two people. Two more."

He gives me a sharp look. "What?" He mutes the television. "Say that again?"

"I opened up the attic yesterday. Iltday. And some kind of a creature got loose."

"You got me about exasperated with that Iltday sh*t." He unmutes the TV punching the button. "About believed you for a split second."

"Gamps it's true!" My lips are trembling and my face feels hot the tears building up there. Again. Soon there won't be any left.

"Skeet I don't have the energy for this right now. Got pins and needles in my leg." He shifts his stump. "Been like that all week what with the storm coming. Come in here and sit down on the bed." I do it and when he continues speaking it's much slower than normal like he was talking to a child. "Now. Listen. Remember when you were a kid and you had started stumbling around slurring your speech and pissing your pants and we took you to the doctor? Maybe you don't. But they found something inside your head. A mass. And well to make a long story short you had an operation a successful one—I mean just look at you look at how far you've come—thirteen years later and no sign of the cancer. But they had to remove a good chunk of brain to get it all out and they told us you'd face some difficulties learning and whatnot. So I've tried to be patient with you and know I haven't been perfect but it seems every day you get up to some new kind of trouble breaking this or that or get some new fancy more outlandish than the previous one and well I'm about at the end of my rope. Can't take it anymore. Can't take another mention of Iltday or talking lawn ornaments or whatever else it is that pops into that bungled head of yours. If only your grandmother were still around. Now there was a lady that knew how to handle you. Or your Mama. Your sweet Mama. I tell you there's no justice in the world Skeet. All the good people gone while that 'By His Bootstraps' *sshole is running around like the big man on campus fathering b*stards left and right. And the rest of us left to rot in a cesspool of filth and sin just waiting for the next storm to come down and pull us all under. Lingdenberry can sell his name and we can't sell diamonds 'cause we're the house the pine tree stabbed. The house with a maimed veteran and a nitwit asylum-case grandson and piles upon piles of sh*t we'll never be able to sell."

About halfway through this speech he begins speeding up his voice slurring till he's talking a streak of nonsense by the end. He's had his share of Brewsters today Gamps has. The smell from the cans is fresh not the day-old beer smell but with a bit of pep still lingering in the air. The bedside table is stacked with them. The floor littered.

I only have myself to blame for his drinking he'd told me once. He was a teetotaler after Korea and churchgoing and honest and a hardworking machinist though he could have lived on disability and Gumma's salary.

"I'm sorry Gamps. I knew I shouldn't have said nothing."

"Always said you were 99 parts imagination and 1 part sense. You saw something you didn't understand and made a monster of it. Next time listen to that voice in your head Skeet Jeffcoat the one that tells you what your Gamps would say." He goes quiet for a while then sniffs and looks over at me with his bleary eyes the milky cataracts reminding me of Russell's glasses and how most of the time you never could see his eyes. People like that are easier to look at. "Someday I'll be dead and you'll have to make do with what I leave behind or else you'll end up some other d*mn fool's problem. Now get me the phone. I think I ought to make some investments."

"Yessir."

I go out and snatch up the red phone with the long cord and think maybe Gamps is right maybe it's like *The Wizard of Oz* maybe it's like I dreamed everything a really bright technicolored dream that feels more real than the world of gray.

Than the dead world of Kansas.

Gamps's Happy Value Shopping voice is coming through the bedroom door and I'm left standing out here wondering what to do. I wonder why he doesn't use that sweet Happy Value Shopping voice all the time it's so relaxing so calming.

In the family room I peek through the venetian blinds at the front yard at the lawn ornament menagerie. "Where are you?" I whisper.

Laughter moves through me or maybe it's moving outside then something up on the roof goes *thunk* and footsteps skitter from the front of the house up towards the center. Makes my skin crawl. I follow along as the sound moves across the house and approaches the hallway and then to the kitchen and on into the laundry room and then beyond the edge of the house.

I open the door and step down into the carport. It's starting to cool down a bit with the storm coming. As I stand out there the wind starts to pick up stirring up a rush in the pine trees the rush like surf all the various bits in our yard creaking and squeaking and groans of metal and the whines of wind moving through broken machines and the rows of shelves. The roof creaks. Maybe the. Wind. Maybe the.

"Who's up there?" I whisper loudly. "Get off our house."

Up. Off.

I wait scanning the edge of the carport roof not wanting to see Her appear. Now I remember how I'd done this before. Listening for. Tracking her. Thinking. I can't. I can't think right. Like there's a stone to push inside me immense and immobile impossible to budge. If only I could think. Think up a plan. Capture Her.

I close my eyes but it's all darkness a red just the red that darkness of closed eyes.

Voices beyond in the other yard. Muffled. I open my eyes and the voices grow louder. Deidre Thomas my neighbor and friend the girl and Jim Byrd as well. They're friends too and why not considering I'm such best buddies with both of them and they work at EAT and come in to rent movies and we all went to Pinehouse High School together. I squeeze my way through the maze of refrigerators to the back of the carport where we got a tangle of PVC pipes that Gamps is going to use for the addition to our house. From here I look over at Deidre Thomas's yard which has a poor empty quality to it. She needs more stuff but what little she has they're moving inside. Her sun lounger where she reads. Patio furniture. Potted plants. Bicycle. She elbows him and he looks up at her then turns toward me and our eyes meet a moment before I look down.

"Hey Skeet!" he calls out. "How's it going man?"

"All right there Jim Byrd." I think he might have been voted Most Athletic in his class. He did play tennis after all and if I already mentioned that I am deeply sorry Ma'am.

He walks over till there's just a few feet between us a few feet of PVC piping and I can examine his sandals and his toenails look like they need a trim. "Diner's closed. Because of Danny. The storm. Y'all heard about that didn't you? Already starting to blow. Anticipate it'll hit in the middle of the night. Did they close down Movie Mayhem?"

I'm not sure if I should nod or shake my head so instead I say. "Well. All right Jim Byrd."

"We're moving everything inside so the wind doesn't pick it up and damage the house. You ought to consider doing the same. Maybe tie down some of your sh*t—uh you know—your stuff."

"I watched that *Conversation* movie starring Gene Hackman and Harrison Ford."

"Oh yeah? What did you think of it?"

"I liked all the saxophone playing and the fact that Mr. Lingdenberry is running for mayor."

"Do you think there was a bug or not?"

"What bug?"

"A tap. You know an implanted recording device."

"Oh. I don't reckon." What bug? I'm still thinking.

"I wondered if it was planted on the saxophone somewhere. You know? It would make sense because the sax *was* him. A piece of him. A window into his mind that became corrupted by paranoia." It's almost like he's not talking to me.

"Well" I say. I am thinking about the pine tree that stabbed our house so many years ago. Remember seeing the perfect way it stuck out at an angle. Like the Good Lord hurled a javelin Gumma had said.

"Anyway. Sorry. You guys need any rope for tying things down?"

"Gamps and I got about a thousand yards of rope" I say then start laughing and Jim Byrd joins in.

"I believe it" he says. "I'm done helping Dee." Deidre Thomas had disappeared somewhere inside when Jim Byrd started talking to me but I can see her at the window in her kitchen looking out at us. "Why don't I give you a hand?"

"Okey dokey" I say but the second the words leave my mouth I feel wrong somehow and I remember that just now something had been crawling around on our roof and laughing. A bug. Her. The foot-thing. "No. You can't. You can't help. You stay over there and watch over Deidre Thomas my neighbor and best friend. It's not safe over here."

"How do you mean? I'll be careful."

"I can do it myself Jim Byrd. But thank you kindly."

"Okay. Just trying to help. Listen. I brought over a gas-powered generator. In case you lose power after the storm we could hook you up. Real simple to use."

"All right there Jim Byrd."

His feet shuffle and I see out of the corner of my eye that he's shaking his head and smiling. "Okay Skeet. Y'all stay safe."

It's Gamps's turn for dinner so he drives us down to the Great Wall which is the only restaurant open Saturday evening everywhere else closed and shuttered even the Willy Nilly's and he picks us up sesame chicken and eggrolls and fried dumplings and pepper beef and fortune cookies.

We drive by the pine woods where Russell's car swerved off the road and crashed and me in it but there's no sign of the maroon Belleville anywhere. Guess I did dream it after all. But Lord what a dream! It's a relief 'cause that means no one died and probably also that I was not fired from Movie Mayhem. Things will continue on as before.

Let me tell you we polish all that food off in no time and read our fortune cookies.

"See what we got here" Gamps says. "'Stay vigilant or else lose something valuable.' What the heck kind of a fortune is that? What's yours say?"

Iltday. It says Iltday Iltday Iltday Iltday Iltday Iltday Iltday Iltday Iltday Iltday Iltday over and over running over the edges of the strip of paper swimming and squirming like worms.

"Well?"

"It says… uh… here Gamps you read it."

Gamps takes it from me and reads the cramped words. "'Do not deny the friend that comes to you in need.'" He grunts. "More advice than it is a fortune. Here. Put them in the fortune jar."

I maybe forgot to explain about our fortune jar which is a normal Calders (Best Cup Is *Every* Cup) 51 oz. can but contains thousands of our fortunes from over the years. Gumma was the one that started the collection don't know why maybe so we could reuse them or something. Maybe when my neighbor and friend the girl Deidre Thomas and I finally move in together and I for a change make *her* pancakes for dinner we can use these and every meal can have a fortune after it.

The Iltday fortune though. Must be Gamps invented something to read some spur-of-the-moment fortune on account of him not believing in Iltday or not wanting to admit that I had been right all along about its existence. But then if Russell didn't die and I wasn't fired from Movie Mayhem then maybe it wasn't Iltday yesterday after all. Maybe Gamps is right. Feel a bit stumped by all this.

I don't know if I want to add this particular fortune to the rest. The words might crawl off it and ruin the rest of the paper strips. Taint the other fortunes.

No.

This one I ought to destroy.

After cleaning up I shred the Iltday fortune and wash the pieces down the sink. Then stare into the drain for some time waiting to see if the words crawl back up and into the metal basin. Something's moving down there. Slick and dark.

There's a knocking at the door and I jump and (I'm sorry to say) cuss.

"Skeet Jeffcoat watch that mouth of yours. And see to the door. I'm not proper."

True enough Stan's off. But I don't want to open the door. Don't want to see what might be knocking there. Don't want to see some long pale leg withdrawing off the edge of the front porch disappearing into the bushes. "Heck Gamps I got cleaning to do. I don't have time to get the door."

"Go on boy." He's watching the portable. A weatherman in a rain slicker being blown sideways.

It's not.

You.

Is it?

I think this. Think it at the voice. Shut my eyes but it's normal darkness behind my eyelids this time and not the red from before. Nothing talks back to me. Maybe she's gone that lady-child-thing is vanished down the drain like the Iltday fortune wet paper fibers grainy melting away.

"Go on Skeet Jeffcoat."

The knocking sounds again more agitated than before. I can see someone standing there through the stiff lacy sun-stained curtain. Not any weird pale legs. But Mr. By His Bootstraps Lingdenberry.

"Hiya there Skeet." He tries a smile but it doesn't catch hold the way his smiles usually do but rather fades into concern.

"Who is it Skeet?" Gamps calls.

"Nobody!" I feel bad saying it. Not just guilty bad but because Mr. Lingdenberry is not nobody. But I don't want any trouble with Gamps like there was last time. A bit embarrassing actually to think about all that. I step out onto the front porch and shut the door behind me. "Gamps isn't proper. That means Stan's off. So you'd better talk with me."

"Skeet. I'm looking for Russell."

I nod.

"I tried paging him but no response. Have got reason to believe he came out this way. I suggested he give you a ride home today and pick up those election signs while he was at it."

Give me a ride home. Then it was true it was real. What happened.

"Yeah. Yeah I know where he's at Mayor Lingdenberry."

He cracks a smile. "Mayor Lingdenberry. Let's not get ahead of ourselves Skeet Jeffcoat." He lays a hand on my shoulder and guides me down the front steps.

"Tell me where he is." He's leading me down the front path when the image of it pops into my head. That stand of pine in the field behind our house where the tobacco shed's at and all those By His Bootstraps signs stashed away the image Deidre Thomas painted and won a prize for back in high school.

"It's. Pretty close. That field. Behind my house." The words aren't mine. Not quite. They feel like someone stuffed them into my mouth. For all I know Russell is really dead but I start talking about the tobacco shed anyway.

"All right. Get in. You ever ridden in a Romulus convertible boy?"

"Nosir."

He puts on his shades and gives me a big grin. "We riding in style today."

I grin back my Pinehouse High School Class of '95 Staying Alive Best Smile secretly wishing I had a pair of shades to pop on too.

We set off down the road the car rocking with the gusts of wind and on the horizon the purple sky is turning the color of Iltday. Maybe because Iltday is coming again quickly on its heels the way it does. Or is it the fact that that storm's nearly upon us? Hanging over everything is a veil of black and gray and purple but that red is starting to eat up the sky. "Did you see our lawn ornament collection?" I ask Mr. Lingdenberry as we near the end of the road and he hangs a left away from town and away from where Russell's car crashed into the woods.

"How could I miss it? Extraordinary Skeet. Just finer than the Emerald City." Mr. Lingdenberry laughs and punches me in the arm. It's strange riding in this car with him and the sky all red beyond his profile. He's got one of those Lolly Pine air fresheners by Auto-Nu dangling from the rearview mirror and even with the top down the smell of the thing makes my stomach turn and I think I might lose all that Great Wall dinner. The car's so loud the way he drives it you barely can notice that he doesn't listen to music when he drives. That's a new one on me. I always like to have music on in the car.

"That's the road there."

"Not much of a road is it?"

It's all bumpy ahead and overgrown. Beyond the bramble-choked dirt road is the rise where the tobacco shed lies hidden by the unchecked and overgrown pine weeds. The hill. The storm is building up over it a massive darkness clawing across the red. I don't. Don't remember Hugo looking like that but then Danny's a Category 1 an entirely different kind of storm. I can't remember is 1 worse than 5?

He inhales deeply. "Just smell that. I love a good storm. Love the aftermath of it. All the trees ripped up and the roads flooded and houses destroyed. If ever you wanted Proof of the Almighty just witness the destruction of His Acts. The insects crushed beneath His Palm. Where am I heading?"

That hill there. I think.

"Skeet?"

"That hill there."

"Don't see any sign of the Belleville."

"The Belleville's somewhere else."

He scoffs at that. I've seen him do it tons of times. Always at Movie Mayhem. Always when talking with Russell. "Can't trust that boy to do anything without me looking over his shoulder. Flunked out of college. A total mess. Got to have his daddy checking up on him every other second." He leans forward over the steering wheel. "That a building in there beyond the trees?"

"Yessir. A tobacco shed. I stashed your By His Bootstraps signs in there."

"And what in the Good Lord's name is Russell doing in there without the Belleville nearby? How the heck's he gonna haul the signs back?"

I don't know how to respond but I think he's just talking without looking for an answer. That's something Mrs. Kelly said people often do. I could say Russell's not here anymore Russell's not anywhere anymore but it wouldn't be right to because Russell can't really be dead can he? I still can't hardly believe any of this is happening.

"Typical. The most inefficient method is the one for him. What did he do? Walk from your house?" The car lurches and something scrapes up against the bottom but the car keeps moving. Then suddenly Mr. Lingdenberry puts it in P and says "This is as far as I dare take it. Might get stuck in this mess."

I nod. "All right sir."

He unbuckles his belt and looks at me. "Well lead the way Mr. Skeet."

I nod. "All right sir."

He kills the engine but leaves the battery on with the headlights shining crooked up the hill. The storm has swelled up and the red's less vivid now. The crickets are screaming and rioting and as we walk the things hop around us like crazy grazing and nicking the skin. A massive flock of birds a dark low-to-earth cloud sweeps across the field and devours the farmhouse in a shivering black mass.

"Storm's got the animals all spooked" Mr. Lingdenberry says.

"Watch out for poison ivy" I tell him. "It's got three leaves—"

"I am blessedly not allergic" he says his voice muffled by a cigarette he's in the process of lighting.

"That's funny. Neither am I. Gamps says it's about the one lucky thing in my life."

The path through the woods is overgrown but it's pretty short and soon we're standing in the clearing amid all the ivy and kudzu that's swallowed the barn. Only a sliver of the headlights reach this far up the hill so they just barely reveal the part where the roof's all caved in.

We stand there. Me staring at the old tobacco shed. I can feel Mr. Lingdenberry's eyes on me. A tingle at the back of the neck. It's quiet for a minute if you don't count all the twittering and sawing of the field critters.

We step inside.

The floor is all pine straw and crawling things and has got that odor of pine resin and earth. The plastic signs lean against the far wall where I'd left them and above is darkness and the broken criss-crossing rafters draped with spiderwebs. Everything is creaking in the wind creaking and popping and groaning.

"Russell! You in here boy?" Mr. Lingdenberry says stepping past me and looking wary from side to side. "I don't get it. I truly do not."

"Don't get what?"

"Why you'd take the signs."

"I-I-I thought it was just a bit of fun. Gamps was having a good time."

Mr. Lingdenberry snorts and spits into the pine straw.

"Mr. Lingdenberry. Can I ask you something sir?"

"Shoot."

"Russell said... he said y'all were going to. Let me go. From Movie Mayhem."

"I'm mighty sorry about that. I truly truly am."

"But you just… you just promoted me to Video Rental Associate two days ago."

"You mean yesterday. I'd be happy to call around to some other places for you Mr. Skeet. Give them my heartiest recommendation. Heck if I can get your vote maybe I could help you find a job with the fine town of Pinehouse." Town. Right. In fact Pinehouse is not a city which is why Gamps always laughs at that Real American City sign. Because it's not a city. That's what makes it funny to him. That's why he says "My *ss!" after it. I get the joke now. Pretty danged funny actually if you think about it.

And that's when I notice the thick veils of spiderwebs lowering from the rafters over Mr. Lingdenberry floating down slowly as if on some crooked breeze. When they pass through the slivered beams of headlight I see they're not spiderwebs at all but pale flesh many knobby jointed legs patched with mold and the toenails all dolled up as Gamps would say. They hang just above his head the feet-things long toes like bird claws just brushing against the top of the slicked-back silver-blonde hair of Mr. Lingdenberry's head. It's not funny anymore.

"M-Mr. Lingden… b-b-berry. It's here."

He swats at the side of his head where a toenail had scraped along his ear.

"The f*ck?" He cusses. Can't believe it. Never have I heard him cuss before. I don't like it don't like him cussing like that like Gamps or Russell no no not Mr. Future Mayor Lingdenberry.

"It's the… the…"

He looks up and screams.

And at that moment the legs which had looked so lifeless come alive and whip around him a claw clamping down on his throat and another planting onto the top of his head the long beautiful toenails of neon-orange Mondays stabbing into his eyes while another seizes him under the left armpit and whisks him up into the dark above screaming for me to help him for f*ck's sake to help him. And God what is it what is it what is it but he doesn't scream long and the sound up there is like a giant egg cracking violently and some kind of hot wet mess splashes down onto the earthy ground a smell of blood and bone and guts steaming all over the By His Bootstraps signs.

Fast as I can I'm stumbling out through the woods and down the hill past the silent Romulus convertible but I see it still every time I blink as I run and I taste him and feel his crumpled body stuffing into the branching tooth-lined gullet of my mouth and think how delicious the iron of blood tastes and the thick hot meaty marrow spilling out of cracked bones is really something impossible to appreciate if you've never tried it for yourself to suck on the arteries of a still-beating heart the surge shooting up through your thousand teeth gnashing thousands and thousands on still-working sensory organs.

I shake the thoughts out of my head and realize all this time that I'd been tasting Mr. Lingdenberry's death I could hear myself screaming in the distance and now my voice explodes into my ears and I cut across through the field tromping over cow ants and through sandspurs and briars.

The rain begins suddenly. Thrashes down. Danny is upon us.

Gotta get back.

Gotta get inside.

Gotta get this connective tissue out of my teeth.

"Gamps! Gamps!" I yell as I burst through the back door.

"In here." His voice comes from the living room and in the background I hear the theme song to *Cops* playing.

"I'm calling 911. It got Mr. Lingdenberry. She ate him. Oh Christ Almighty!"

I try this phone and that phone in the hallway but none of them are working. Gamps appears in the doorway. "What's all this commotion about?"

"The thing came in on Iltday. Her. She. She ate him."

Gamps rolls his eyes. "Who ate what now?"

I shake my head at him. No doggone use telling him. I try each phone again my mind working but running up against that block in there that leap I can't make that keeps me from doing the right thing the smart thing. I slam the telephone into the wall screaming and it crashes through the drywall and the phone the red one the working one the one for Happy Value Shopping calls comes away in pieces dangling together on wires and coils of metal I didn't know were inside it like the veins and flesh I've got stuck in my teeth when I blink.

"What the h*ll you do that for? I'm the only one round here knows how to fix drywall. Thank you very much. More work for me. More work for Gamps. It's endless with you. The sh*t I have to put up with like Job his-d*mn-self…" His voice and the sound of *Cops* dwindle away to nothing as I stare at the hole in the wall and the hole in the house in the roof where the pine tree broke through that storm that Hugo storm that had brought with it the first Iltday the first time I could see the entire rainbow for what it was. The full spectrum of days a truly beautiful thing and there had been scratching scratching scratching before Iltday came but me so young I had always been afraid and hidden in my bedroom. Heck wasn't till I was a full-grown man and a high school graduate when Iltday rode in a second time with Hurricane Allison in '95 Staying Alive. That was when I came out and opened the iron door with the honeycombed surface and let Her into Pinehouse and led Her to Mr. and Mrs. Lyles then Ms. Elsworth then…

"I killed her" I say. "It was me. I did this. It was my fault Gamps."

"You're not making sense Skeet. Plug in the other phone. I gotta call that doctor of yours. Dr. Wen."

"The phones didn't work then either. Before Gumma died."

"Skeet you're freaking me the f*ck out. Get in the living room and sit down. Let Gamps handle it."

I shake my head. "I gotta do something. Gotta stop Her."

"You gonna sit your *ss down like I said."

"Where's your gun Gamps? The 12-gauge pump-action shot-gun."

The back door swings open and cold air surges through the kitchen and into the hallway bringing with it plastic to-go bags and containers like styrofoam rodents scurrying this way and that. Then the door slams shut and everything grows still again. Gamps hobbles into the kitchen doorway and peers inside and I see him from two perspectives suddenly staring at his side from here and then glimpsing him in the red doorway looking in at me. It is identical to what happened with Gumma except that the house was so much neater then but otherwise it feels like a picture of the past is painted over the present. That's what this all is like time folding upon itself events matching up a kind of symmetry. Was it Her that said that?

"Something's there" Gamps says squinting.

"Gamps. It's Her. It's that... it's I... I don't know what." I go and grab his arm. Try to pull him away.

"It's all shadow in there." He raises his voice threatening-like. "You get out now you hear! I'm getting my gun. Anyone here when I come back is gonna get a face-full of buckshot."

He limps past me and down the hall towards the bedroom and shoulders open the door and disappears inside.

As for me I hesitate at the doorway and work up the courage to look in and just as I do the back door swings open again and this gray form slinks out into the rainy dusk before the spring returns the door to the frame with a whack.

"Where did they go?" Gamps calls to me.

I close my eyes but it's all dark out there now and I can't make sense of where it's going. "I don't know!"

"Fear not." Gamps is back with the shotgun slung over his shoulder. "Thieves and marauders coming out in the storm thinking they can take advantage of civilians in their time of distress." He pushes past me and into the kitchen.

"Gamps let me have the gun. You're not stable on Stan."

"Not on your life boy. You're not stable in the mind so we'll risk it with old Stan here."

"Don't do it Gamps. It's dangerous. It ate Russell and Mr. Lingdenberry."

He cackles. "You mean Mr. 'By His Bootstraps' and 'By His Bootstraps' Jr.? Good riddance to them!"

"It ain't a burglar dang it. It's a-a... a monster."

"You mean a monster like the wandering psychopath that killed your grandma and the Thomases? All the better. Get in your room and lock the door. Everything'll be fine and dandy in a moment." He turns on the light in the back hall and his eyes rove over everything and so do mine thinking there might be some trace left behind like a colored toenail a patch of moldy skin. Something.

The linoleum creaks under Gamps as he reaches the door. "Go on and git Skeet. Gamps'll be just fine."

In my room I take out my notebook and colored pen and click it onto Saturday purple then click it over to Iltday red and then back and forth and back and forth and back. Purple fish swim before my eyes but red streams are dripping down the walls and pooling on the floor to the point that I don't know what day it is anymore. But I have to do something have to decide what day it is what to do what what what.

I rub my eyes and blink and it's darkness all of it and I hear laughing the high-pitched laughter of a child in my ears. And muffled is Gamps's voice calling out for me to "Come on out of there! I can hear you!"

I've written something in my notebook:

by Skeet Jeffcoat Deveaux by Skeet Jeffcoat Deveaux

Over and over in alternating red and purple letters.

"Lord Jesus!" I say aloud why can't I think this through why can't I just once break through the wall in my mind? I press the pen to the paper and close my eyes and in that peaceful dark a door swings slowly open a door I'm looking out of as Gamps passes by. The roar of the storm fills my ears. The entire carport is flooded with rainwater and mud and I reach out and grab hold of Stan and jerk on it right as he's taking a step through the muck. The prosthesis yanks loose and Gamps tumbles onto one of the stacks of mini refrigerators.

He's cursing as I creep out of the stale moldy interior of the fridge I'd been stuffed inside all octopus-like. And when our eyes meet his go wide with fear and he starts stammering nonsense and raises the shotgun to fire but I'm too fast and kick out at him with one of my legs and knock the gun down just as it fires.

There's a burst of light and fire. A splatter of blood and bone and Gamps screams at the sight of his exploded foot. Then I scramble over onto him and reel him into me with my eight legs.

My eyes pop open and I gag at the taste of Gamps's blood. I'm in my room pen in hand clicked onto Iltday red a wall of mattresses surrounding me. Rain is thrashing down and the wind is howling the house rocking and swaying. I get up my knees knocking against each other and leave the room. As I pass through the hallway I hear something crash down and feel the earth shake. In the next instant the lights flicker off and all the appliances and AC wind down. Everything is bathed in darkness and throttled by the roar of the storm. Takes a moment for my eyes. To adjust. Then I notice light streaming in from the living room window a tentative light at the end of the hallway everything gray and undefined in here.

Something crunches under my feet. The remains of the red phone.

At the entrance to the kitchen I can make out the sound of someone screaming nearly drowned out beneath the torrent of rain. But just audible. If I close my eyes the sound is suddenly louder than the rain and it fills me up my skin vibrating with the terror of my victim making the tiny hairs and goosebumps stand up on my skin. The struggle improves the flavor like a dash of salt.

I open my eyes and shake the image out of my head the sound muffled once more the moisture lifting from my skin.

All the kitchen knives we got are plastic take-out ones. There's a tool cabinet and a few boxes in the back hall which have screwdrivers and hammers and other useful things. I pick up that hammer with the claw broken and I remember now how it broke how two years ago I had swung it into one of those legs the one with the Iltday-red nails as the lady-thing had been in the process of eating Gumma. Hit it so hard the metal chipped like a tooth and left one of Her legs forever crippled. Destroying the symmetry of both creature and tool.

I turn the handle and the door flies open and smashes against the side of the house sucked out by the storm. Outside it's a black-and-purple roaring haze and the treetops are all rocking and swaying and threatening sideways. All the shelving and lawn equipment and pool tables and everything has begun to tumble towards Deidre Thomas's house piled and confused together and a tree has uprooted and crashed down on the tool shed which is nothing now but a smear of splinters.

The wind is screaming around me and if Gamps is out here screaming too I sure as heck can't hear him. I yell for him at the top of my lungs but who knows if he can hear it. I go down to the carport which is now several inches deep with rainwater and the rain is blowing sideways in a barrage of stinging needles.

I just catch the sound that crunching of bone and I close my eyes by accident. It's an unfortunate time for that because suddenly my throat stretches wide and there's Gamps's body halfway down it. Going in leg first with the shotgun still clutched in his hands but his eyes all white and lifeless and streams of blood spilling down over them and drenching his beard. In the background there I am hunched over vomiting amid the refrigerator graveyard.

I open my eyes and look up from the vomit washing away in the river of rain and there She is a spider of eight legs long with the painted toes and the one shoe and some of the feet deformed and shorter than the rest with tiny baby toes and all these legs angling into the body or head (for it's only a head) an upside down one with lips stretched impossibly wide like a feeding boa constrictor ready to receive the body of Gamps and its almond-shaped eyes paler even than its skin paler than pearl paler than blue-sky clouds.

I see this in an instant but it's a long instant. A frozen time like Iltdays with the rain stalling around us in streaks then this hiccup in time clears itself and She gobbles up the body in sped-up motion and the gun splashes into the puddle. I jump forward swinging the damaged claw of the hammer but She's too fast squeezing away through the crevice between two refrigerators with a billowing of all Her legs just how an octopus would jet away from its predators in a nature documentary.

The child-lady-thing giggling in my head.

—Now. Skeet. Shame. On. You. Didn't your Gumma teach you better than that?—

You *ate* Gumma! And Gamps and and Russell and and Mr. Lingdenberry future Mayor of Pinehouse—

—I'm protecting you from them Skeet from these people that devalued you that used you that looked down on you that mocked you. Don't you see we need each other? I need you when the storms come. I need you to observe Iltday and to open the door so I can keep building the pattern and add to the dimensions of symmetry. I feed on its perfection. I'm already feeling so much stronger. And you need me to clear your mind to fill in the hole they cut out of your brain and to destroy all those that laughed at you in their hearts. Without our connection your mind would barely function. You used to be worse off you know before I lent you… some of myself.—

I trudge forward through the rush of water and floating treasures. The rain and wind raging so hard you could feel it inside like when the bass is too loud on the stereo or you're standing at the West Main railroad crossing with a train speeding past. Takes me a moment to find it but my fingers circle around the barrel of the shotgun and I drag it out of the mucky water.

—And I've saved the worst for last. The worst offenders. Perfect additions to the pattern.—

"What's worse?" I scream. "Worse than Gamps? There's nothing worse than you taking my Gamps!"

There's a loud groan and squeal vibrating through my body then suddenly the roof of the carport peels off and flies into the night like some kind of giant mechanical bat. I climb up the stacked refrigerators and peer across the roof and down between my house and Deidre Thomas's and the yard is nothing but rapids churning out towards the road. She's dancing across this river in the strangest way a floaty way without seeming to touch anything a kind of puppet on strings. Bobbing and barely seeming to grace the muddy froth of water with her delicate toes. I take aim with the gun but She's out of sight around the front corner before I can fire.

The front corner of Deidre Thomas's house.

My neighbor.

The girl.
And best friend.
And more.

I go back through the house and stuff the hammer in my belt and get out a flashlight. Out the front door I see that Sumter Road which is at the bottom of a small hill has transformed into a lake with waters choppy and thrashed by wind and rain. The lights across the street flicker shining only weakly through the torrent. A pine tree had caved in the front of the house across the street and the roof of their SUV and on our side of the street it's nothing but blackness and storm. I drop down into the front lawn and get soaked up to the knees in cold water and my combat boots keep getting stuck as I move and it feels like lugging buckets of water. Seems the current could carry me away any moment.

Closer to Diedre Thomas's house I see that the front door has been smashed in. I ring the bell of course but it doesn't do anything because the power's out. It smells like Deidre Thomas in here smells clean and like roses or some other flower I wish I could name.

She doesn't have a lot things is what I notice first. There's a couch and chair and television and a shelf with books and a stereo but we got about ten or more of each of those things. I wish I had known. Wish I had. Could have helped her out sooner. Shared what we had. All our things. All our life.

It's such an empty place and clean with all kind of room to move around in. I could lie down on the floor. I could sleep in the danged living room for Christ's sake. What I realize is I've done this before have come in here following the same lady-thing into this house when She came here to murder Deidre Thomas's parents. But I was too late and then Iltday came again.

I stand there in the living room and listen to the house. Hard to hear anything over the constant drum of rain and howling of wind and creaking of trees outside and the groaning joints of the house. I pass the flashlight over the room and my flashlight catches something on the coffee table. A cassette. One of those "Achy Breaky

Heart" mixtapes I made her. The one stained with coffee and egg. She kept it after all.

Something moves over to the right and I scan the wall of the living room and as it passes across a doorway I just see it disappearing into the darkness long and ghostly and skinny. I hadn't noticed or thought about those legs how they're about as long as a person is tall maybe longer long enough that it'd scrape along the ceiling so danged gangly long. It doesn't make any kind of sound the same way some tiny insect wouldn't like a spider gliding over the floor towards the heel of your foot to climb up it to climb up the back of your leg and into your jean shorts.

I see you.

——*I know Skeet. Close your eyes and watch.*——

I step towards the doorway and find a hall branching left and right a leg vanishing around to the left. That gimp one dragging a bit all shriveled up and about to rot off but the Iltday-red nails still bright and eye-catching.

"Hello! Deidre Thomas! This is Skeet Jeffcoat Deveaux your neighbor and friend and more! Gamps is dead but don't worry! I'm armed with his pump-action 12-gauge shotgun!"

——*Close your eyes and listen. They heard you Skeet. They are saying unkind things. You scare them and disgust them. Watch me add them to the pattern.*——

I keep moving forward. Don't listen to Her. Don't listen. Don't.

But when I blink I see a door creaking open into a small bathroom and Jim Byrd and Deidre Thomas are huddled in the tub with blankets and pillows and flashlights. And when they shine them up at me their eyes go wide and they scream.

Then I'm running down the hall and when I turn the corner I see the flashlight beams flashing this way and that through the bathroom door and what looks like a forest of bony legs dangling down from the ceiling. Jim is strung upside down. Half of him stuffed inside of the mouth. A look of shock twists his face even as he beats the thing in its blank pale eyes with his flashlight.

One of the naked legs has Deidre Thomas pinned down in the tub and she's struggling and wriggling beneath it like a live copperhead in a sack before you watch Gamps beat it senseless with a shovel.

I raise the gun looking down the mud-caked barrel. A piece of rebar or something is jammed in there and right before I fire something pricks at the back of my mind something about the mud or the barrel I don't know what. I point at the underbelly of the thing at the mouth there the thin-lipped mouth and the pale eyes but I can't get a clear shot with Jim Byrd's torso hanging out like some giant muscular tongue.

So I aim instead at the leg pinning Deidre Thomas the girl my neighbor and more.

And I pull the trigger.

Chapter 9
Iltday

I'm blinded and my ears are ringing and the bones are vibrating in my arms. It takes a moment before the ringing subsides (and even then one of my danged ears isn't working properly no matter how many times I press it into my shoulder) before the dim beams of the flashlights register again. The bathroom window is shattered and the storm is wailing in. Blowing big shards of glass onto the floor. My nose is filled with the sharp burn of gunpowder and heat and the fresh smell of the hurricane. Their flashlight beams have grown still one of them in the tub and angled at the ceiling and the other lying on the bathroom tile illuminating the severed leg of the thing. A messy separation but without any blood. Just rotten frayed flesh. But still moving. Squirming around on the floor. Flopping here and there.

I start to pump the shotgun when I notice that the barrel has transformed into a skeletal umbrella. Still smoking. It exploded. The barrel rayed and twisted into metal skewers.

I stare at everything in confusion. So quiet except for the ringing. In my ears. Ringing. The storm is like something on the TV. When you have to turn it down so Gamps can make a call to Happy Value Shopping. Like Dorothy's storm.

And the moaning. Something's moaning.

Deidre Thomas. The girl. And neighbor. And everything.

She's doubled over in the tub and rocking. Jim Byrd's gone. The thing has gone too. Must have fled out the broken window. Left behind its dismembered leg though. The thing caresses my calf and I kick it away from me into the dark corner behind the toilet.

Then I approach Deidre and crouch down in front of the tub. Her hair hangs dark over the edge and is thick and wet as mud.

"Deidre. Deidre Thomas" I say and reach out to move her hair. My hand seems to be shaking but whether it's from the blast of the gun or the nerves in me I couldn't say. It is wet. Blood. I can smell it. Though it looks black and unlike blood. Like from an old horror movie before color made it glow.

I part her hair slowly. Looking. Looking at the blood streaming down the lip of the tub. Then lift her head. She looks fine she looks like I remember from the picture in the yearbook our Pinehouse High School Class of '95 Staying Alive yearbook. She looks just like she did in that picture. Smiling her half smile. Eyes a little narrow. Lips quivering. But there's something new a skewer of metal sticking out of her forehead and it dribbles a bit dribbles blood down her face in a perfect straight line. Down the center and over her nose and across the lips of her smiling mouth and down the point of her little chin and drip drip dripping into the tub.

"Deidre Thomas I'm here for you." I touch the metal twisting out of her head. Hot. Touch gently. "That's okay" I say. "That's just like where I got my scar. I don't know if you ever noticed. My scar." I brush my wet hair off my forehead and touch the scar where I've seen it so many times in the mirror. "If you looked closely at my forehead. There's a bit of a scar there. Where I was cut open. Don't know if I mentioned."

Deidre Thomas's lips part. A rasp escapes her. A sound from deep within her chest.

"You're all right now." I help her out of the tub. She's got on a blue tie-dye t-shirt and sweatpants and she's a little wobbly but I lead her out of the bathroom her arm linked through mine and the hand of her other arm reaches across and finds mine the one still holding the base of the exploded shotgun barrel which is even now still hot. In the other I got the flashlight and I train it down the hallway. On the ground out there the leg is inching along and slips around the corner. The one with the banana-yellow toenails.

The ringing in my ears still hasn't faded but I can see all right.

The house is rocking and swaying. Lightning crackles and the bare house lights up in gray and red the thundercrack painful it's so loud.

Deidre Thomas rasps "Ssskeet."

"Yes Ma'am. It's me. Skeet Jeffcoat Deveaux. I made you those 'Achy Breaky Heart' mixtapes and the audio recordings of *The Wizard of Oz* and a billion dang stories. That was me" I say leading her through the darkness.

Through the battered-in door the wind blasts in cold and wet and as we get nearer I feel it and know it will be coming. Of course.

Iltday. Coming the second time. It always comes. Twice.

And that thing. She. Will be making Her way to the pull down. Back to where She came from that world of bone and dark.

"Now that we'll be living together we can listen to 'Achy Breaky Heart' every day and watch *The Wizard of Oz*. Gamps is gone now but you can put up in his bed or we can make you a new one with one of my mattresses. I got a bunch of mattresses I don't know if I mentioned that to you. I could sleep on a different mattress every danged day of the week. Iltdays included."

"Ilt… Iltday" Deidre says. Parroting a bit. The way I do sometimes. When my mind grows really cloudy and thick. But for once everything is clear. What was it She said? She lent me something? I guess it's true that sometimes I think clearer than others. Like clouds passing through the sky. Sometimes dark and sometimes light.

Suddenly the wind dies down and a light streams in through the open doorway.

It's a red light. Deep red and bright.

"Beautiful isn't it?" I turn to look at her my neighbor and best friend the girl Deidre Thomas. Her face is bathed in the red light and the black blood dripping down is branching across both sides of her nose now and branching again across her full lips. "I bled too"

I tell her. "I bled a lot when I was cut open. In the hospital I mean. That's what Gamps says anyway."

Then I realize as I'm looking at Deidre Thomas that she's not jittering the way Gamps and other people do when I find them during Iltday. She's standing there her body a little slack with her eyes rolled up in their sockets and her eyelashes fluttering and her hand clutching mine. But she isn't jittery and she isn't an X-ray like Gamps and everyone else always is.

"Deidre Thomas this is Iltday. This is my special day. The color red. You can see it can't you? You see it this time."

She moans.

"And the colors of the week? Maybe you can see them too."

She moans.

Iltday has calmed the storm and washed away the clouds and rain. Practically every house has been damaged to some extent. So many pine trees have been bent or flattened. Deidre Thomas's house survived at least and so did a couple others but not many. Some looking worse for wear than the old tobacco shed.

Our house fared no better. Iltday usually transforms it into an elegant mansion but not now. Our small ranch has been crushed beneath a massive tree that came down right along the peak of the roof. Its branches are wedged all up inside it pushing lush fans of pine needle out through the windows and through a new fissure down the side of the house. Where my bedroom was and all my millions upon millions of words were written and all my recordings and all our treasures. It's even worse than Hugo all those years ago.

Everything smells of rain and fresh-snapped pine and the chemical innards of houses the insulation and treated wood. But it also smells of Iltday that unpleasant smell that's been dogging me all week. The earth has vanished leaving all the piles of ruined houses floating above the churning red-and-black under-skies. And rising out of the ruin of our house is the marble staircase spiraling up and up and up to an iron door suspended in the sky. I hear something flexing and rattling and then notice Her clambering up an angle of siding blown out from the wall and leading up to the roof of our house which has now become a strange bumpy and cracked and splintered terrain. Soon She reaches the base of the stairs and starts slithering up them.

All the shelving and our treasures from the backyard were tossed and tumbled by the wind into the lane between our houses creating a crooked bridge of sorts leading from Deidre Thomas's front porch to Gamps's and my place.

I lead Deidre Thomas down her front stoop and we step onto the bridge. We inch across shelving and over pool tables and the upturned bellies of lawnmowers and even Gumma's old Novi hatchback all of it swaying and twisting beneath our weight. I get Deidre Thomas to dig her hands into my belt and follow along behind.

Halfway across I hear something behind us and see the severed leg following along.

"Look at that" I say.

Deidre Thomas does not look. But I watch for a few seconds as the thing bunches itself up and then reaches out then bunches itself up again. "Isn't that funny Deidre Thomas? Isn't that funny the way it moves? It's like a caterpillar."

She moans. She basically does that whenever I say her name or talk to her.

"Well. Let's keep on moving then."

We cross and the leg follows. It would be nice to go out and have three Double-Braggers with Cheese please fries and Bragger-sized Atomic Fizzes Neon Lime Flavor (Fear the Fizz) but it's not a work-day as you know and what with the storm I don't think that will be happening. "Or I could fix some Bubba Joe's (Hear That Sizzle) Ultra Thick Cut Bacon and Waffacombs Now With Superhex Syrup Pockets with plenty of syrup or hey Deidre Thomas you can make your pancakes like they have at EAT with the butter that comes in scoops like an ice cream scoop. Now that you and I are living together and I got my promotion at Movie Mayhem I reckon I could buy EAT. No. Wait. I forgot I'm not going to be working at Movie Mayhem anymore. I was fired and then Mr. Lingdenberry was eaten so I don't know what will happen to Movie Mayhem. It would be a good story anyway about how I got rich working at Movie Mayhem and decided to buy the restaurant EAT where Deidre Thomas the girl and my neighbor works but she doesn't know it's me that buys it then I give you a raise so that you make one thousand dollars an hour and also make you famous so that everyone in the world will know how wonderful you are. Then one day Gamps and I (but Gamps was eaten too but never mind 'cause he wasn't eaten in the story) we watch TV and see that Deidre Thomas got an award for Best Waitress and she wanted to thank God and Jim Byrd and her mother and most of all Skeet Jeffcoat Deveaux 'cause really you knew it was me all along that helped you and also 'cause you knew it was me that wrote that book that was your favorite and your biggest inspiration not to mention all the 'Achy Breaky Heart' mixtapes."

By the time I stop talking we reach the house.

"What do you think about that story Deidre Thomas? Gamps says most of my stories are BS."

She moans staring off into the distance. I don't know if a moan is the right word. There's something a bit distant about it. Very quiet and almost as if it's not her voice. I'll be honest with you I don't know if I like it very much. I liked her the way she was before she got the metal sliver stuck into her forehead. But I can at least wipe the blood out of her eyes and face. I noticed she was blinking a lot blinking the blood out of her eyes and making bloody tears of them.

"Maybe you need a cigarette. Did you bring your cigarettes?"

She moans.

"Well I don't know what that means. Forget about the doggone cigarettes I guess. Let's go on up the stairs." The creature no longer as fast-moving as it was during the storm is still climbing up and up and they seem taller than I remember disappearing into the scarlet above us.

I help Deidre Thomas climb the slanted side of the caved-in wall and then across the ruptured roof to where the stairs rise out of the wreckage completely untouched by the storm. Then I hear behind us a scratch scratch scratching on metal. I sit Deidre Thomas down and hustle back to where we came up the toppled side of the house and see the leg down there toenails making slow drags down the siding trying unsuccessfully to pull itself up.

I got to admit I feel pretty bad about it since I did shoot the thing off so I lower the barrel of the exploded shotgun down and scoop it up by the knee that's closest to the ankle. It turns and flops a little but I manage to reel it up to the roof and carry it back over to Deidre Thomas. So helpless the thing isn't scary as it once was. Just a bit weird I guess.

"It seems to want to go up the stairs too" I say noticing how it reaches out for the marble.

Deidre Thomas doesn't notice the leg which is all right because it smells terrible it smells like our house did when the squirrel died up in the attic and where the leg was severed the torn frayed flesh is squirming as if all those bits of skin and muscle and nerves and blood vessels are thread-like worms. I manage to get my shotgun through my cowboy belt and heave the leg over my shoulder and then help up Deidre Thomas and we walk hand in hand up the steps.

She stumbles a lot.

"Clumsy" Gamps would say.

But I help her along because Gamps was clumsy too. Same as me. We're all a little clumsy sometimes.

As we climb I see above us how the stairs have changed. Turning in a square spiral then going on up in another direction. I can just make out. Her. Far above us

Where are you going? I think.

She doesn't respond.

She stopped talking to me ever since I shot Her. It makes sense if you think about it. In All-Star Class with Mrs. Kelly we learned a trick about people that I do use sometimes when I find myself confused. And it's this: If you don't understand what somebody wants from you or why they are acting a certain way you can pretend you are them you can put yourself in their shoes you can imagine you are doing what they are doing etc.

And if I imagined I was this lady-thing and someone named Skeet Jeffcoat Deveaux shot me with a shotgun and blew one of my legs off I don't think I would want to talk to him anymore thank you very much.

We climb and you can hear strange sounds below us earth cracking and water rushing out through the holes. When I look down I see that our street has vanished into the lava under-skies of Iltday. There's nothing remaining now but this staircase and us and the sky and the faint low-pitched crackling it makes and the smell of old blood and this rotten leg.

Deidre Thomas I learn is not very good at climbing stairs banging her shins here and there and stumbling forward. She almost lands on her face one time almost jabs that sliver deeper into her skull but I catch her before it happens.

Her green eyes are a little easier to look at now that they've rolled up in their sockets some and you can see the fine red blood vessels of her eyes like delicate cracks in the pavement. Looks a bit like that Marilyn Manson t-shirt Russell Lingdenberry liked wearing. Except this is Deidre Thomas the most wonderful girl in the world.

By the time we reach the top of the stairs my throat is parched and my chest heaving and all sweaty. Even in Iltday the humidity is something powerful. At the top platform we find Her curled up and motionless like some kind of human spider that died in a dark corner. One leg is dangling across the latch. The latch I see now is designed to fit the strange shape of the foot. Well that makes sense I suppose.

Poor thing couldn't get home. Died right on the threshold.

One of Her toes twitches.

Maybe She's not dead.

"Excuse me. Wake up Ma'am."

Her eyelids flutter a little bit the lips quivering.

"I brought your leg back. I'm sorry and all. About blowing it off with the shotgun."

Life stirs in the curled-up legs and She makes several attempts to rise.

"Don't. Let me help."

I grab hold of the body head part a kind of inverted human head with the legs sprouting out of what would be the neck and forehead and bending down so it can walk proper. I'll be honest I don't rightly understand why She's built the way She is. Maybe it would make more sense if I went through the door and lived with Her for a time in that strange dark place She came from. That's the kind of thing Mrs. Kelly would say to our All-Star Class.

She stands. Trembling and shaking.

—*Thank you Skeet… but I'm dying. I was unsuccessful. The pattern was incomplete… asymmetrical… this act and the one that came before. The deaths don't align in space and time and memory.*—

"I reckon not. Anyway I got your leg. Seems like it's still alive. Maybe they can reattach it for you. I mean if you got doctors where you're going. I'll get the door for you I guess." Gumma taught me about opening doors for the fairer sex by which she meant ladies and while she never mentioned lady-things I reckon it still applies. Well I open it and a cold dry air pours out.

The lady-thing scoops up the severed leg with one of Hers and staggers through the door. Beyond are the wheels of bone grinding away a vast machine which when I look at them again seem almost like clouds.

It's Her sky I'm gazing at.

And I'm not afraid at all.

No Ma'am.

It's a beautiful thing.

By Skeet Jeffcoat Deveaux

Afterword

From: Dr. Alan Jefferson
Date: August 18, 1998
To: Dr. Carla Wen
Subject: Deidre Thomas

Dear Dr. Wen,

Thank you for sending me the manuscript. Despite its questionable reliability, Mr. Deveaux's writing has been most illuminating with regards to the treatment of Ms. Thomas's disordered behavior. Her progress initially was quite good, but as of late she has begun to regress into a delusional and frenzied state. The parallels between her and Mr. Deveaux's disorders are uncanny: she hoards books and everything else imaginable in her room and grows extremely agitated when the staff try to help her declutter; she has become a prolific journalist; and most striking she mentions Iltday and the colors of the week. An excerpt from her diary can perhaps best illustrate said parallels:

During rec time today I watched Weather-24 in the day room and made notes about the progress of Hurricane Bonnie but Nurse Fran made me put on soaps because talk of the approaching storm was upsetting the other patients.

Idiotic soaps washing away their anxiety while a storm is bearing down on us. I just sat in the corner and colored in the pages of my diary. Colored so hard I ripped the pages.

Dr. Jefferson came around with his team of note-taking lackeys and they were all very interested in why I was coloring today's page gray. It is interesting. Because I seem to remember a time when Sundays weren't so gray. They were starchy-dress days. Kneeling-in-the-pew days. Body-of-Christ-melting-on-the-tongue days.

Dinner was that tough meatloaf and grainy mashed potatoes and soggy vegetable matter Thursday green. Same meal every Sunday. I've tried to explain to the kitchen staff about the colors of the week but they don't understand.

As I poked it with my plastic fork I heard that sound again that's been bothering me these past few days. A scratching sound. Sometimes slow and dragging. Other times frantic and desperate. I tracked it down to a bend in the wall in the west wing. It's funny but… I could have sworn there used to be a door here.

I wish we could know for sure what happened between Mr. Deveaux and Ms. Thomas following the end of the Hurricane Danny Murders. The manuscript you provided suggests that Mr. Deveaux may have imparted some of the details of his delusions upon Ms. Thomas after she sustained her injury, and, considering the parallels in their psychoses, it's possible that some elements were ingrained on Ms. Thomas's psyche during her vulnerable state. I would appreciate any more information you have on Mr. Deveaux's treatment plan—i.e., his drug regimen or anything else you managed to glean before the recurrence of his cancer and subsequent death. I will, of course, continue to update you on Ms. Thomas's progress. As the only surviving witness of the murders, her testimony will be crucial to putting this investigation to rest. In the meantime, we've had to keep her restrained and sedated. Ever since the Hurricane Bonnie state of emergency came into effect, she's been obsessed with opening doors, even doors that don't exist.

Regards,
Dr. Jefferson

Acknowledgments

Thank you first to my wife, Dongfang, who read many drafts of this book over the years during its journey into novel form. Thank you also to my grandmother, to whom this book is dedicated; my parents for (among other things) sending me to writing camp when I was in high school; and to all the various family, friends, and mentors over the years that have encouraged me to write and helped me to improve. Last but not least, thank you to David Sula, my editor, for his belief in the book and the many invaluable ideas he brought to the table during the editing process.